IN THE TWEET OF THE NIGHT

In the Tweet of the Night

True crime stories from a small-town bird reporter

SUSAN TOWHEE

Towhee Tales

COPYRIGHT

Towhee Tales Publishing, 2023

First edition print ISBN - 979-8-218-15136-2
First edition ebook ISBN - 979-8-218-15137-9

Towhee Tales Publishing
Nashville, TN
towheetalespublishing@gmail.com

DISCLAIMER

Any references to real people, real places, characters, company names, or historical events are used fictitiously.

DEDICATION

Dedicated to Mom and Dad

RESTFUL ROOST MAP

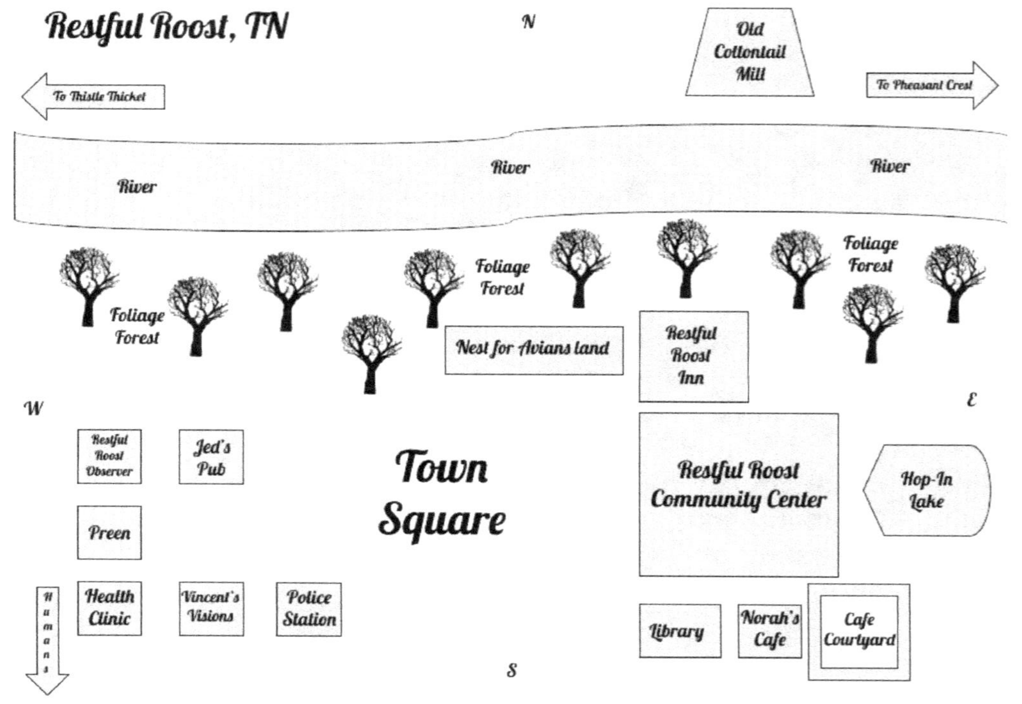

RESTFUL ROOST RESIDENTS

Susan - Eastern Towhee *Pipilo erythrophthalmus*
Adam - Eastern Towhee *Pipilo erythrophthalmus*
Joe E. - House Finch *Haemorhous mexicanus*
Simon - Song Sparrow *Melospiza melodia*
Nick - Northern Cardinal *Cardinalis cardinalis*
Katherine - Great Blue Heron *Ardea herodias*
Norah - White-breasted Nuthatch *Sitta carolinensis*
Marilyn - Mourning Dove *Zenaida macroura*
Andrew - Mourning Dove *Zenaida macroura*
Goldy - American Goldfinch *Spinus tristis*
Mary - American Robin *Turdus migratorius*
Charlene - Carolina Chickadee *Poecile carolinensis*
Thea - Northern Bobwhite *Colinus virginianus*
Chad - Northern Cardinal *Cardinalis cardinalis*
Vincent - Black Vulture *Coragyps atratus*
Jed - Pomarine Jaeger *Stercorarius pomarinus*
Tammy - Northern Cardinal *Cardinalis cardinalis*
Alex - American Crow *Corvus brachyrhynchos*
Dewey - Eastern Chipmunk *Tamias striatus*
Evelyn - Eastern Cottontail *Sylvilagus floridanus*
Hopper - Eastern Cottontail *Sylvilagus floridanus*
Peter - Pileated Woodpecker *Dryocopus pileatus*
Vanessa - House Sparrow *Passer domesticus*
Millard - Mallard *Anas platyrhynchos*

THE STORIES

INTRODUCTION

Well-manicured lawns, riverside views, a bird feeder in every yard, trees perfect for nesting, and no cats! Sounds like the perfect environment for a bird, right? Think again!

The pleasant and charming town of Restful Roost turns sour when unsavory characters appear to cause mayhem and mischief.

What follows in these pages are true tales of nest invaders, thieves, ghosts, political corruption, and murder!

Come along with me, a bird reporter for the local newspaper, as I entertain you with tales from my town.

Welcome to Restful Roost!

~ 1 ~

COWBIRDS FROM HELL

The Story (as I remember it)....

Around 4 a.m. on April 2 I was awakened by a buzzing police scanner with a CRM (Criminal Mischief) call at a nearby cardinal nest. Thinking this was probably some sort of spousal squabble, or even a late April Fool's Joke, I pondered if it was really worth the effort (Restful Roost really has no crime so I assumed this was a false alarm of some sort), but, a job is a job, so I said goodbye to my mate, Adam, and grabbed my notebook and pen and flew off. The cardinal nest was near the edge of town so it took me a good minute or two to fly there. Upon my arrival I was met with gore and bloodshed!

I spotted Police Chief Joe E. Finch on the scene and I headed over to get the deets.

Joe was one of New York City's finest detectives in

his younger years. Remember the name Maurice "Black Quill" Gianto? He was a crow family mobster who ran the illegal feather trade in Panama. Well, Joe was the cop who brought him down in a raid at a NYC port. Dumb Black Quill decided to visit his mother for Mother's Day. Joe had his connections, found out about the visit, and was waiting for him.

Soon after the arrest and conviction Joe contracted the nasty finch eye disease. Lost an eye and his job. He also found the bottle. After a year or so Joe decided police work was still in his blood, so he cleaned up, found the opening for a police chief here, and he made the move.

Back to the story!

Joe held a wing up and told me to stop and not to get any closer.

Chief Finch: "This is nothing a little lady should see."

I told Joe it's my job to be there and he can't withhold basic information from me. I also told him to stop calling me "little lady." He laughed and filled me in.

Chief Finch: "Female cardinal; name is Tammy; leaves nest around 3 a.m. to search for nest material; gone only five minutes she says; comes back to find one of her eggs destroyed; in its place is another egg; ID unknown of new egg; destroyed egg is shattered and beyond hope; little lady is so distraught; her husband, Nick, is sitting on the nest now until she calms down."

Me: "Holy Toledo Joe! Nest predation in Restful Roost?"

Of course, we have heard of these things happening in other places, but not here. I thanked Joe for the info and let him be as he had quite the job to do.

I walked over and surveyed the scene. The egg was cracked in multiple places from the fall. Yolk spilled out on the grass. I saw my cousin Simon Sparrow finishing up his reports. He works at the local clinic and helps with forensics from time to time.

Such a travesty! My heart ached for Tammy Cardinal. I would talk with her later. Now just isn't the time for a nosy reporter.

The following questions ran through my mind:

Where was Mr. Cardinal when this happened?

Was Tammy being watched?

How often did she leave her nest?

What bird did this? I bet it was a cowbird. Nasty buggers!

What will happen to the new egg? Surely Tammy can't be expected to raise it!

By that time, quite the crowd had gathered. I decided to escape the commotion and flew up to the nest to have a chat with Mr. Cardinal.

Me: "Hello, name's Susan Towhee, reporter for the Restful Roost Observer. So sorry about what happened today. It is a travesty and the perp will be brought to justice!"

The cardinal started to cry.

Me: "So sorry! I didn't mean to upset you again!"

Nick: "It is all my fault."

Me: "Your fault? Why on earth would you say that?"

Nick: "Because... I was out all night...um...drinking and if Tammy hadn't left the nest to look for me, our nest wouldn't have been violated."

Me: "Ah, so Tammy left to find you?"

Nick: "Yea."

I didn't know what to say. It was kind of his fault. That guilt is on him. Still, the perp had to be caught!

Me: "I truly don't know what to say to comfort you, but I am on the case and so is Chief Finch."

I said my goodbyes to Mr. Cardinal and decided to visit the local pub later when it opened to verify the story. Pub owner Jed Jaeger was friendly towards the press, so I knew I could count on him for the details on Nick's drinking.

Next, I flew to my Restful Roost Observer office to file my breaking news story. My workaholic editor, Katherine Heron, was already in the office. Be careful not to piss her off! She is known to spear things in the office with her beak when she gets angry. After a quick review she approved it to run that day in the morning edition.

NEST PREDATION HITS RESTFUL ROOST

by Susan Towhee - Published April 2, 2022 in
the Restful Roost Observer

Police were called to a nearby nest belonging
to Tammy and Nick Cardinal yesterday morning
with reports of a disturbance. According to
Police Chief Joe E. Finch, an unknown bird laid

an egg in their nest and destroyed an existing egg which was laid by Mrs. Cardinal.

Details to follow on what will happen to the non cardinal egg.

Chief Finch says this is a classic case of nest predation and wants the public to please call the Restful Roost Police Department at 55-TWEET if you have any information or tips.

Stay vigilant Restful Roost!

After posting my story, I flew to my nest to see if my mate Adam wanted to grab lunch with me. Hopefully he was home. He is the landlord for nests in a few trees nearby so he could be busy with a random early morning request from a tenant. I had to fill him in on this!

Back at home I found Adam tending to our nest.

Me: "Hey hon, you hear the news?"

Adam: "Nope, been working on some properties this morning and haven't seen a soul. What happened so early this morning?"

Me: "An egg was destroyed in a cardinal nest! Chief Finch thinks it is a brood parasite at work!"

Adam: "You're kidding! Here in Restful Roost?"

Me: "Not kidding. Personally, I think a cowbird did it."

Adam: "A cowbird? Haven't seen them around in ages. How did he get to the nest? Where were the parents?"

Me: "Daddy bird was getting lit at the pub, apparently. Momma got worried and went to find him. That's when it happened."

Adam: "How horrible!"

Me: "Agree. Do you want to join me for lunch at Jed's Pub? I want to do some sleuthing there and confirm some details."

Adam: "You betcha! I have been craving a worm sandwich."

Me: "Perfect! Meet you there at noon. Since they are meeting today, I am going to fly over to the library and meet up with the book club group to see if anybird has more news."

Adam: "You mean see what new *gossip* there is?"

Me: "No comment."

The book group meets once a week early in the morning at the library near the Hop-In Lake. One of the reasons we call our town Restful Roost is because we are nestled so close to a river, which is a treasure for any small town. The river supplies the fish eaters among us with plenty of food and allows goods to arrive and leave by boat efficiently. We have ample shade with our Foliage Forest and many well manicured lawns to visit and forage on. Since the river is a favorite spot for citizens, the town decided to build a community center nearby. The center has large rooms for events and a concert hall. The Restful

Roost library is located right next to the center. In fact, most of our town is all in one small area. It is truly a Restful Roost! I digress...as I flew to the library, I saw the entire group from the window. The members are Norah Nuthatch, Marilyn Dove, Goldy Goldfinch, Mary Robin, Charlene Chickadee, and town librarian Thea Bobwhite. That week's book was *I Know Why the Caged Bird Sings*.

Me: "Hi ladies!"

"Hey Susan!" they all replied.

A little background on the ladies:

Norah Nuthatch owns the very popular Norah's Café which is right next to the library, attached by a courtyard with a lovely seating area. Her café serves all types of delicacies that she prepares herself including a variety of suet cakes, seed trail mixes, spiced mealworms, flavored insects, etc! Herbivores and omnivores are welcome there! The café is the only breakfast spot open in town.

Marilyn Dove is the town mayor's (Andrew Dove) wife and when she isn't busy reading, she is gossiping!

Goldy Goldfinch is the top realtor in Restful Roost. She owns Restful Roost Realty. They say if she handles your nest listing it will be sold by the end of the week. Luckily, Adam and I are happy where we are and have decided to keep our nest for life, but we do work with her to list our properties for rent.

Mary Robin is the town doctor. She is also a huge bookworm and seems to know a little about everything. She runs the local health clinic in town.

Charlene Chickadee is the events coordinator at the Restful Roost Community Center. I don't know what connections she has, but Restful Roost always gets the best artists to come to town. Birds fly from miles around just to see one of our sold out shows. I hear she even booked the Australian Superb Fairywren superstar *rachel* for our New Year's Eve show! Yes, *rachel* only goes by one name now. The name is not to be capitalized and must be italicized.

As mentioned, Thea Bobwhite is the town librarian. With a few questions she can determine exactly what your book style is and pick out just the right book for you. We say it is a gift!

Goldy started in on me as soon as I entered the library.

Goldy: "Did you hear the news this morning, Susan? Oh I am sure you did. Tell us what you know!"

Me: "Oh yes, I was on the scene. One egg was laid and another was forcibly removed from the nest. Total damage, no hope for repair. Nick Cardinal was apparently out drinking and Tammy left to check on him. By the time she was gone, the deed was done."

Mary: "Simon took a photo from the crime scene. It's a Brown-headed Cowbird egg."

Gasps went up from the group.

Thea: "Hold up, how do you know that is a cowbird egg? Eggs usually all look the same!"

Mary: "I just know. I minored in oology in college. They have a habit of laying their eggs in many species' nests. The sizes are pretty much the same, but the pigment markings are subtly different. I bet if the female flew off with the other egg instead of destroying it, Tammy wouldn't have known the difference. Until the egg hatches of course."

Norah: "Do the cops have any leads?"

Me: "Not sure. Going to head to the station next to see if the chief knows anything."

Goldy: "That Nick! Out drinking while his wife sits on a nest. Sounds like my no good husband."

Marilyn: "I heard Nick has a girlfriend on the side. A young cardinal that just moved to town. If I ever found out Andrew was chasing tail feathers, his bags are packed!"

Norah: "Oh, Marilyn, no one has to worry about that, Andrew is respectable."

Charlene: "Besides, if word came out that Andrew was cheating on you, he would be voted out of Restful Roost in a heartbeat! Speaking of, has anybird heard if Andrew will have a challenger for the mayoral race?"

Marilyn: "Hadn't heard. Andrew's approval ratings are in the 90's so we feel pretty confident, but the news of this crime could hurt us."

Me: "So what is this cardinal's name who Nick might be canoodling with?"

Marilyn: "Oh honey, I would hate to give out her name, especially if it is just hearsay."

Five seconds passed.

Marilyn: "Her name is Janice."

Norah: "With that big bald spot from molting I don't see how Nick can attract her or any lady for that matter!"

I had to interject with a defense for Nick.

Me: "Oh those grow back! And I really doubt Nick is that way. I just didn't get that vibe from him. I do think something else may be going on. I am sure Tammy has to leave the nest occasionally. Sounds like she was being watched and targeted."

Marilyn fluttered her wings which caused a whistling sound.

Marilyn: "Watched and targeted? Oh my! Andrew should call a town meeting on how to handle this."

Trying to change the subject Charlene brought up new shows at the community center.

Charlene: "I sure hope they catch him or her before our big shows start. We have the Chuck American Black Duck concert on April 22."

Me: "Oh I love him! Who else have you booked this summer? Can you say?"

Charlene: "Well, I can tell you the Valentino Vogelkop Superb Bird-of-Paradise confirmed last night!"

Gasps arose from the group.

Thea: "I cannot believe it!! He is sooo talented!"

Marilyn: "Wait, who?"

Mary: "Marilyn, you gotta look him up online. He has the most extravagant mating dances you have ever seen. All the ladies in Restful Roost will be at this show."

Me: "What is this about *rachel* performing on New Year's Eve?"

Charlene: "Still in the works! I hope to have the full schedule complete by the end of spring."

Thea, hoping to steer the discussion back to the reason we were all there, walked to the front of the group.

Thea: "Ok birds, we need to focus! Now, what did each of you think about Maya's book?"

Along the way to the police station, I thought I saw

Chad Cardinal. The bird flew to a nearby tree with a lot of messy and noisy construction going on. Chad works with Vincent Vulture who is the town contractor, so it had to be him. Might be wise to see if he knows anything, Hell, he might be related to Tammy and Nick.

Me: "Hey Chad, got a minute?"

Chad: "Oh hey, Susan! Sure thing! Got a few minutes left on my lunch break! Was just at this really, really nice feeder on Maple St. It had like 5 feeders with fresh berries, sunflower seeds, thistle, ..."

Me: "That sounds yummy Chad. Sorry to interrupt, I don't want to keep you too long. Did you hear about the commotion this morning?"

Chad: "Oh yea, my uncle really messed up this time. He won't get out of the doghouse with my aunt for a while!"

Me: "I see, Nick is your uncle. Happen to know where he was when the nest incident happened?"

Chad: "Probably at Jed's, but I can't say for sure."

Me: "He did say he was out drinking. So what are you building here?"

Chad: "Fancy two story nest for some rich couple. It's a vacation home. Pretty sweet, huh?"

Me: "Seems more economical to build your own nest."

Chad: "Well, if you got the money, why not? Uncle Nick has the property reserved next to this one for an even fancier nest!"

Me: "Is that so? When were they expecting to move in?"

Chad: "The plan was after the little ones were born and after his *big deal* came through."

Me: "Big deal? What is it that Nick does again?"

Chad: "He is unemployed now, but he kept talking about something big that is going to make him a millionaire! Wish I had a piece of that! Hey, I better get back to work or my boss will have my beak."

Me: "Alright, thanks Chad! Thanks for talking with me and so sorry about your cousins."

Chad: "Thanks. Later!"

A "big deal"? I wonder what Nick was up to. Maybe this was what he was doing instead of a tryst with a supposed girlfriend. And a millionaire? Maybe over the hill in bourgeois Pheasant Crest, but not here in Restful Roost! The only rich family in town is the Cottontail rabbit family. Something fishy was going on.

When I looked at the time I saw it was already close to noon so I had to hold off on my police station visit.

Jed's Pub was crowded, as usual. Adam had a seat saved at the bar for me and was already nursing a beer. It was probably his favorite, an Old Speckled Hen.

Adam: "Find out anything new?"

Me: "No, just speculation that Mr. Nick Cardinal may have had a side bird and might be involved in some shady business deal."

Adam: "You're kidding!"

Me: "Not kidding!"

Jed walked over to take our order.

Jed: "The usual?"

Me: "I guess, since there is no variety on the damn menu!"

Jed: "Hey! I ain't feeding my customers seeds and berries. Go to a birdfeeder if you want that. You come to Jed's and you get real food."

Adam: "Jed! Some birds only eat seeds and berries!"

Jed: "Well not here. I get quality proteins delivered daily. I serve birds who are too busy to scratch around and search for their lunch."

Me: "What about something a little different like those hot meats sunflower seeds? They are infused with habanero chilies!"

Jed: "Sounds uppity."

Me: "Ugh! Ok two worm sandwiches please."

Jed: "Coming right up!"

Jed was difficult, but he means well. He is a Pomarine Jaeger and not from around here. His breeding habitat was the tundra, which was ok since he likes the cold, but Jed hated life at sea during non-breeding months. I met him a while back at a Terror Tern concert in St. Louis and told him about our town. He visited one day and never flew back North. Said his dream was to open a bar one day. Jed bought a vacant store for real cheap and painted the whole thing black. The food menu came when he decided he didn't like some of the food options in town. He was an Arctic bird after all and an omnivore. Thankfully, he does not have a taste for bird meat.

Me: "Say Jed, did you hear about the disturbance this morning?"

Jed: "Yep, I heard it through the grapevine. Hate that it happened to Nick."

Me: "Nick said he was never drinking again."

Jed: "Well damn, there goes my best customer!"

Me: "Jed! You shouldn't say such things! It is a good thing he will lay off the booze. What time did he leave last night?"

Jed: "Was never here."

Me: "What!? He said he was out drinking all night!"

Jed: "Well it wasn't here. He usually is most nights, but I didn't see him at all last night."

Interesting. There was only one bar in town. If he wasn't here, then where was he?

Since this raised even more questions, I knew my next stop had to be the police station after lunch. No distractions this time!

Arriving at the station around 2 pm, I found Chief Finch was about to fly out the door.

Chief Finch: "Hello Susan! Had lunch yet? Was about to fly to the thistle feeder on Sycamore St. to fuel up. Maybe you can fill me in on what you scratched up."

Me: "Just ate, but will be happy to fly with you."

After a short flight a block away, I filled him in on my conversations and findings so far that day including that Nick was not drinking at the pub, that he may have a side bird, that the egg most likely belonged to a cowbird, and that this may involve a potential business deal gone wrong.

Chief Finch: "Hmm. Seems I may need to hire you for my team."

Me: "We are all on the same team on this one chief! Besides, I don't look good in a uniform."

Chief Finch: "Ha! Now, you say you confirmed with Mary Robin that the eggs were from a cowbird? Well, I made a few calls to some friends up north and they said this all sounds like a scam that's been going around with cowbirds in their area. They lure birds away from their nests so they can easily parasite their broods. Keeps their populations growing all while they do no work. How they do it, I don't know."

Me: "So this could be a nationwide deal?"

Chief Finch: "Yep, but we can stay on top of it if we keep our peepers open. Be sure to keep me abreast of anything new!"

Me: "Will do. I'm on my way now to chat with Tammy. The sooner we can figure this out, the quicker she will find comfort."

We said our goodbyes and I headed back to the scene.

I found Tammy in her nest when I arrived and she was still in a bit of a daze.

Me: "Hi Tammy. Susan from the Restful Roost Observer. So sorry to hear about what happened here. You ok to talk to me for a few minutes?"

Tammy: "Uh, I really don't think I am up to a conversation right now."

Me: "I know Tammy, but we have to find who did this, and if we can help Chief Finch figure it out then we can prevent this from happening to other birds."

Something must have clicked in Tammy and she started squawking at me.

Tammy: "I just can't talk about it! Leave! You are harassing me!"

Me: "Ok, ok, I will leave. I didn't mean to upset you."

Tammy started to cry again, so I made my exit.

Geez Louise, that did not go the way I wanted, I thought.

At that moment I heard rapid *po-ta-to chip* bird calls from behind. Sounds like a goldfinch. I turned to see Goldy Goldfinch flying towards me. Something must have happened!

I flew towards Goldy and we perched on a nearby tree.

Goldy: "Susan! Where have you been?"

Me: "I just finished harassing Tammy Cardinal apparently. What's wrong? What has happened?"

Goldy: "I saw a cowbird!!"

Me: "WHAT? Where?"

Goldy: "This afternoon at my Pilates in the Pines class. I looked up and saw one looking at us. So creepy!"

Me: "Are you sure?"

Goldy: "Yes! After the library meeting I went home and googled images of them. It was definitely a cowbird! And he had a notebook with him and was writing furiously. Susan, he was looking at all the women in the group. Remember what you said earlier that they were watching and targeting Tammy?"

Me: "Strange! Did you tell the chief?"

Goldy: "I will as soon as I find him! The pilates class

members discussed meeting tonight at Norah's Cafe. I am worried he will be there, too."

Me: "We should go and keep our peepers open, and also warn the other ladies to be on the lookout."

Goldy: "Sounds good. 6 p.m. is when the meeting starts."

Me: "Meet you in the tree across the street. Be there early!"

It was 5:45 p.m. and Goldy and I were ready for spying in the oak tree across from Norah's Cafe. From what we saw everybird was already at a table and being served pastries and coffee. Norah stayed open late on the nights special clubs met.

Me: "I told the chief that we were here in case something happens."

Goldy: "Good thinking."

A bird approached us from behind. "CAW CAW!" That could only be one bird. Alex Crow had spotted us.

Goldy: "Alex! Shut up! We are on a stakeout!"

Alex: "Oh, I am so sorry! What are we looking for?"

After filling him in on our plans and the news of the day, he agreed to hang with us on the branch for protection.

Alex: "If I see that cowbird try anything I swear I will peck his eyes out."

Alex was new to town. He had just moved to Restful Roost from Miami to take care of his mom. He also just opened up a new salon called Preen which specializes in feather dyeing, nails, and massages for the residents in town.

Me: "What are you doing here Alex?"

Alex: "Well I thought I would join the pilates ladies club tonight and catch up on juicy gossip."

Goldy: "You don't even do the pilates in the mornings. Oh wait! Shh - look! I think I see the cowbird. Yep, that is the same one I saw this afternoon and he has that damn notebook again."

Me: "What could he be writing?"

We watched for a few minutes and saw another cowbird approach. That bird said something to the other bird and they both flew off. About that time Chief Finch arrived.

Chief Finch: "Sorry ladies, I was doing an interview and got here as fast as I could."

I explained what was happening to the chief.

Me: "We saw a cowbird watching the ladies from the window!"

Goldy: "And it was the same one I saw this afternoon watching us at my Pilates class."

Alex: "He was taking notes and another cowbird was with him! You missed him by seconds!"

Chief Finch: "Very dangerous to be doing undercover work ladies, and, uh, Alex, but, good job! Can you all please come by the station and make a statement? Maybe help us with a sketch so it can run in the paper tomorrow?"

We all agreed to go right then.

Goldy: "Sure thing chief! Anything to get these creeps off the streets."

"Look, I don't know nothing, but I know my rights! This is police harassment!"

That's what Chief Finch said Nick said to him when he was being interviewed. The chief recounted the story to me over a cup of coffee in the police station break room.

Chief Finch: "I told him to calm down and that this was just another interview and that he wasn't under arrest. I just wanted to know where he was out drinking that night. Nick starts wailing and then breaks down and tells all. Said a bird told him he would make millions. It was part of a new development deal in town. The bird told Nick that the details were incomplete and all Nick had to do was meet him that night and sign some papers. Said if he didn't do as he says Nick would be pushing up daisies with other birds who double crossed him. So when he gets there the bird says Tammy needs to also be there to sign the papers because Tammy and Nick have a joint bank account. Nick flew to get Tammy. When Tammy arrives she asks too many questions, then the bird gets angry and tells them both to get out and the deal is over."

Me: "Did Nick say what he looked like?"

Chief Finch: "Yea, gave a description for what looks like a cowbird. Once Goldy and Alex are done with the sketch I will show it to him. He also gave me the coordinates for where he met the bird. I went out to check on it, but no bird nor evidence was there. Just an old abandoned junkyard. My gut says he is telling the truth, but I have asked Tammy to confirm the details."

Me: "Sounds like a scam artist. Mind if I run these developments in tomorrow's paper?"

Chief Finch: "Go for it."

COWBIRD IS CONFIRMED AS THE CULPRIT

FRAUD SCAM ALERT

NEST PREDATOR SUSPECTS SPOTTED

COWBIRD EGG FINDS NEW HOME

by Susan Towhee - Published April 3, 2022 in the Restful Roost Observer

Attention residents of Restful Roost! Your help is needed. Police Chief Joe E. Finch has confirmed the identity of the nest predators in the April 1 incident. Brown-headed Cowbirds! According to victim Nick Cardinal he was approached by a cowbird and asked to take part in a development deal in town. He was lured from his nest, along with his wife, Tammy Cardinal, to finalize details. Chief Finch thinks the plan was to get the birds out of the nest so the cowbirds could lay their own eggs without distraction.

Residents of Restful Roost: be on the lookout for suspicious characters asking for your investment in business dealings. These cowbirds may be working with others to fraud you! Call the BBBB - Better Business for Birds Bureau to verify information.

A mysterious bird was also spotted gawking and taking notes at two separate female groups yesterday. The bird has since been identified as a male Brown-headed Cowbird. Chief Finch says the suspect may be armed and dangerous. The perp may also be working with a female cowbird. Call 55-TWEET if you see any suspicious activity.

The cowbird egg in the cardinal nest will be carefully removed by the organization HUB (Home for Unwanted Birds) and relocated to a special incubation home in New York.

Stay vigilant Restful Roost!

I awoke around 4 a.m. and decided to fly to my office at the paper. Might as well see if any new developments came in. Upon my arrival I found my boss Katherine Heron already at work in her office. Katherine's work ethic is the main reason why the Restful Roost Observer has won the best newspaper award in the South for the past 3 years. Also there was Dewey Chipmunk, freelance photographer for the paper, and one of the most irritating creatures alive. I greeted them both.

Me: "Hey Katherine, what time did you get here? And hey Dewey."

Katherine took a sip of coffee, probably her fifth cup. I spied the coffee pot and saw it was almost empty.

Katherine: "Didn't leave last night. Too busy."

Dewey: "Oh hey Susan! Say, I didn't hear from you about the nest murder. I gotta hear about these things if pictures are needed."

Me: "I just took notes, Dewey. Photos of the incident couldn't be printed anyway."

Dewey: "Yea, but I have a brand new Nikon. No photos on a major news story? Tisk, tisk Susan! That isn't quite up to the standards we need at our paper is it, Katherine?"

Could this creature *be* any more annoying?

Katherine: "Whatever Dewey. Susan, hopefully with the confirmation that the criminal is a cowbird running in today's paper we can get this case closed. If Chief Finch doesn't catch this fool soon we will have more nest problems and an infestation here. No matter if it is in their nature to defile other nests, we can stop it! Go ahead and take the day off. With all the excitement of yesterday I am sure you need extra rest. Dewey you can go home, too. I don't even recall asking you to come in today."

Me: "Thanks Katherine and be sure to get some rest yourself!"

I hurried out the door before Dewey could follow. It is times like this when I love that I can just fly away.

With permission to leave work, I headed home. Our nest is at the base of an oak tree. I built it a while back in only 5 days. The nest has a strong base of oak bark strips and twigs from multiple local trees. It is lined with pine needles and the softest grass I could find. However, it does need repairing every so often and Adam and I do as best as we can.

Our family has since moved on and lives all around the south. Thankfully, we haven't lost any eggs in our broods. Adam and I are well aware that cowbirds can take advantage of towhee nests and we are grateful we made the decision to halt brooding. Now is the time to enjoy semi-retirement and each other more.

A short flight away is the river and the town Pheasant Crest is to the east. To the west is Thistle Thicket. Towards the South is the home of the humans who supply ample amounts of birdseed and water in their yard to supplement our daily foraging needs. I noticed that the owners of all these houses really like to watch us while we eat. Not sure why humans like to look at us so much. Are we really that interesting? And why do they put free food out for us? Some yards have cages small birds can fly into and feed without distraction of potential predators or a squirrel interrupting their meal. Very nice of these humans to consider that we like to dine in peace! Some birds think humans are gods and we should worship them. I don't know about that. I see some humans dragging canines on leashes, so they must not be all that good.

I spent the day relaxing and made a quick dinner of

roasted grubs. Adam surprised me with the news that a pool was going to be installed. Imagine! A quick swim every evening under the moon and stars. What a life! We opened a bottle of Blanton's and settled in to watch a couple episodes of *Quantum Migration* (love that Scott Beakula!). I went to bed around 10 p.m. and hoped for a full night's sleep.

That was not to be...

I was awakened by pecking from Goldy around 2 am.

Me: "What are you doing up this late? What's wrong?"

Goldy: "My husband was acting odd. He said he had to meet a bird. Something weird is going on."

Me: "Something weird is always going on with him."

Goldy: "No, something even weirder is happening, I know it. I checked and our bank statements and checkbook are missing."

Me: "What?? Didn't he read the article in today's paper to watch out for financial schemes? Idiot! Let's go find him!"

We flew together around the town high up so as not to be spotted. After a minute or so we found Goldy's husband at a dumpster outside Jed's Pub. Gross!

And he was there with a cowbird!

Goldy: "I can't believe this fool has an envelope with him. Is he really going to sign something over to that bird!?"

Me: "We should go wake up the chief and tell him about this."

Goldy: "I am not leaving until I find out what is going on. I am going to drop kick both of these bird brains."

Me: "Please don't. The cowbird looks mean and he might be working with others."

Goldy: "You mean that other fool behind the dumpster?"

I looked and saw another cowbird, this one a female by the looks of it.

Me: "So he does have a partner. Let's hope they aren't armed like Bonnie and Clyde."

Goldy: "I am going in."

Me: "Noooo! You must be patient. Wait... what's that shadow?"

Goldy: "It's Jed!"

Jed rounded the corner with a steel baseball bat. He knocked the female out, turned and knocked the male out. All in one turn!

Goldy's husband flew away as soon as the melee started.

Goldy: "Fool."

By this time armed agents had arrived and wingcuffed the still blacked out perps.

Busted!

——————

COWBIRDS CAUGHT

by Susan Towhee - Published April 4, 2022 in the Restful Roost Observer

The Restful Roost police department is pleased to announce an arrest has been made in the nest predation case. Two Brown-headed Cowbirds, a husband and wife team named Eric and Ann Cowbird were arrested for the crime. The scheme was a plot to trick females into leaving their nests so the cowbird could lay an egg and remove another. Birds with similar colored eggs as the cowbird were targeted. A notebook was found with detailed notes on breeding females in the area. Once the sketch of the cowbirds and description of their actions were distributed to law authorities, the FBI (Federal Bird Investigators) took notice and sent agents overnight to Restful Roost.

The cowbirds were caught late last night behind Jed's Pub in the middle of another deal and were arrested by the FBI. According to an unnamed FBI agent, the cowbirds were wanted on money laundering and nest development fraud charges in multiple states. Now with the added charge of nest predation, the couple will likely face life in prison.

The town of Restful Roost would like to thank Goldy Goldfinch for spotting the cowbirds

behind the pub and Jed Jaeger who incapaci-
tated the perps seconds before the agents
arrived. "I heard chirps outside my bar and
called the cops. I did what I had to do to protect
my fellow citizens. They have been kind to me
since I moved here. It was the least I could do,"
said Jaeger.

I suppose in the end Nick only wanted a better life for
Tammy and his brood. They have since packed up and
moved to Vermont to be closer to family.

Goldy Goldfinch, Jed Jaeger, and I were given Good
Citizen awards for our help in spotting and reporting the
cowbirds to the authorities. Goldy also threatened to di-
vorce her husband if he tried one more dumb move with
their finances. Since the incident he has not returned
home. Goldy hasn't lost any sleep.

Just another day in Restful Roost!

~ 2 ~

THE CRAZED CACHING CHIPMUNK

The Story (as I remember it)...

10 p.m., awakened yet again by my police scanner, this time with a THFN (Theft Now or Just Occurred) call. Location was Norah's Café. I knew the café was closed because Norah only leaves the café open at night for special events and those usually end by 9. Since Norah bakes the café's morning baked goods she has to get to bed early. I knew I had to check this out, not only for the story, but to check on my good friend.

I arrived at the café a few minutes after the call to find Police Chief Joe E. Finch was already there taking notes while interrogating Norah. I saw no evidence of a break in or damage of any kind. The chief caught my eye and waved me over.

Chief Finch: "This town is worse than NYC with this crime wave!"

Me: "Well, I hardly call two incidents a crime wave, chief. Norah, what exactly happened here?"

Norah: "This is all so horrible! I felt energetic tonight so I decided to work on inventory in the basement. I hadn't checked on things since my last delivery two weeks ago. I noticed a huge mess on the floor. Seeds spilled everywhere and empty containers. I don't know what to do! My entire summer supply is gone! I will be out of business in a week!"

Chief Finch: "Look little lady, this town takes care of its birds. You will get through this and I will find who did this and bring them to justice."

While I was confident we would catch the thief, I was not so confident the chief would be the one to do it. Many in town felt like he was losing his touch a little bit. Maybe he wasn't expecting such activities in our small town after his big city experiences. However, now was not the time to bring up the police department's shortcomings. By police department I mean just the chief as he has no deputies. Have I mentioned we are a small town?

I calmly peppered Norah with questions because I wasn't sure the chief would ask or had asked.

Me: "Look, Norah, I will do a write up on this for the paper. Is there anything you can tell us that might help identify the perp? Have you had any upset customers lately? Any birds out there jealous of your success? Scorned lovers?"

Norah: "No, I honestly have no idea who would do this to me. Rather, who would do this to the town? I feed many birds daily. Birds rely on my quality seeds! I have insurance, but it will take a while to replenish my supply. Chief, will you dust for prints and check tracks outside?"

Chief Finch: "Well, I am doing all I can, but the thing is, there are no tracks. I can't determine how a bird could have gotten in or out."

Me: "Hold up, maybe it wasn't a bird at all."

Chief Finch: "Holy cow, you think a mouse could be responsible? Don't you keep traps here, Norah?"

Norah: "Of course I do! But the traps are empty!"

Me: "Don't worry Norah, we will figure this out."

I left for the office to file my story after consoling Norah and helping her clean up a bit. It was true, she had lost all of her supply. More than that, she lost her sense of security.

THEFT REPORTED AT NORAH'S CAFE

ENTIRE SUMMER FOOD SUPPLY LOST

by Susan Towhee - Published June 11, 2022 in the Restful Roost Observer

A major theft was reported to the Restful Roost police department last night at Norah's Café. Owner Norah Nuthatch informed the Observer that her entire summer seed supply was stolen in the event. "In one night my business was ruined," stated Nuthatch.

Police Chief Joe E. Finch has no leads or a motive. If anybird has information related to this case please call Call 55-TWEET. Chief Finch asks all Restful Roost residents to lock their doors and set mouse traps until the perp is caught.

Stay vigilant Restful Roost!

Back at the office I brought up the idea for an expose in the paper on how understaffed the police department was.

Katherine leaned back in her peeling, faded leather chair.

Katherine: "Let's see how long it takes the chief to solve this case. The problem may be with him and not staffing."

Me: "Sounds good. I will put that idea on the back burner and wait to see what happens."

Katherine frantically started opening all of the drawers in her desk.

Katherine: "WHERE THE HELL ARE MY PENCILS? I ORDERED A CASE LAST WEEK!"

She squawked so loud the birds in Thistle Thicket could hear.

Me: "Come to think of it, I haven't seen them recently. Hey, Dewey! Come help me look for them!"

Dewey ran in from the break room with his cheeks stuffed.

Dewey: "Hey, I am on break now. It really isn't my job to keep track of things around here."

Katherine walked over to him and stared him down.

Katherine: "Dewey, your attitude has been horrible recently."

Dewey: "I am, you know, like, really under a lot of stress right now."

Katherine: "STRESS!? What stress? You haven't submitted any photos lately and you show up late!"

Dewey started to tremble and ran away crying.

Me: "Geez, what is the deal with him lately?"

Katherine: "No idea, but I am really not a fan of his now."

Me: "How about a lunch at Jed's to get away for a bit?"

Katherine: "Sure. Maybe I can remember where I put those damn pencils after I eat. Let's fly."

As we entered Jed's Pub we saw a full house.

Katherine: "Quite the crowd here today. Oh hey, there is Charlene talking to Jed. Let's sit by her."

We walked to grab the last two seats at the bar.

Jed saw us approaching.

Jed: "Yep, with Norah's Café closed for the day I am getting the brunt of her customers. Picky bunch who want seeds and nasty fruit!"

I rolled my eyes.

Me: "Well that is what their typical diet consists of! You

know what, no sense arguing with you on this again and again. I will have water and a worm sandwich please."

Katherine: "Make it a fish sandwich for me."

Jed: "Coming right up!"

Charlene: "Susan, such horrible news to wake up to today!"

Me: "Yes, it was quite the crime scene. I know Norah will rebuild her inventory and get back on her feet soon."

Charlene: "We should help somehow. What about a food drive? I can fly around and be the town crier on the details as well as post something at the community center."

Katherine: "Love that idea! Susan, write up a plan and we can print it in the paper tomorrow."

Charlene: "We can also do some sort of show ticket giveaway, too. I will send details later."

Jed arrived with our food.

Jed: "I overheard and I would love to help. I can't do this another day with double the customers showing up. Susan, let the birds know in your story that I will provide free beer and snacks if they drop off a box of food."

Me: "Wow, that is very generous! I will definitely add that. The community, and Norah, will especially appreciate it."

Jed: "Yep, and talk to that useless police chief and see if he can figure out who did this. I plan on sitting up tonight with a shotgun to protect my bar tonight."

Jed looked up and saw a customer.

Jed: "Hey Alex! I got your food ready. One sec."

Alex Crow peeked in between me and Katherine.

Alex: "If you ask me, I think the chief is ready for his retirement in Hawaii."

Katherine: "Wait. What? Retirement? Hawaii? I thought this was the chief's retirement spot?"

Alex: "Well, while grooming his feathers he confided in me that he just wasn't feeling it here and wants even nicer climates. He let it spill about Hawaii after his third complimentary champagne. I offer those during spa treatments, by the way."

I got my notepad out.

Me: "Well that is big news. Can I quote you on this?"

Alex: "Oh no! I have already said too much. You cannot repeat that!"

Me: "Fine, but keep us posted if you hear more gossip."

Alex: "Well, since the chief seems to be distracted by future luaus and palm trees, how about you and I poke around at Norah's and see if we can find anything?"

Me: "Sure! Meet you there in an hour?"

Alex: "Yass!"

Norah was still cleaning up when we arrived. Alex and I found her in the basement.

Alex: "Hey Norah, mind if we look around for clues?"

Norah: "Of course not! Any help is appreciated! The chief has no leads and hasn't been back to look around himself."

We went back outside and walked the perimeter looking for clues. Then we flew around the top of the building.

Finding nothing new we decided to go back to the basement where the theft occurred.

Alex: "Holy cowbird, Susan, look at all the empty boxes! No kidding that she lost a lot of seed! There has to be a clue here somewhere."

Me: "Let's check the corners."

As Alex approached me his claw clipped the corner of a box and he tripped and tried to steady himself on a nearby shelf. The shelf began to topple.

Me: "Move and fly!"

Alex: "CAW CAW!"

Alex flew to the top of the room and the shelf crashed to the floor.

Norah flew into the basement.

Norah: "What happened? Everybird ok?"

Me: "Yes, just a clumsy crow is all."

Norah's eyes caught something in the corner.

Norah: "Hold up, what is that hole in the floor?"

With the shelf now on the floor, a visible hole could now be seen where the bottom of the shelf stood.

Alex: "Ladies, I think we have found the smoking gun."

Walking closer I examined the freshly dug dirt.

Me: "Yes, this could be the entrance and exit hole, but what could have done this?"

Alex: "Eww, what if it is a rat?"

Norah: "Oh gross! I will get shut down by codes for this!"

Me: "I am going to fly and tell Dewey to stop by and take photos of this for our story. Norah, can you fly to the police station to alert the chief?"

Norah left and Alex flew with me.

As we entered the Observer office I spotted Dewey reading a comic book with his feet on my desk!

Me: "Hey Dewey. Can you please get your paws off my stuff!? I need you at a crime scene to take photos. Can you head over now, please?"

Dewey: "Very exciting! Sure thing! Where at?"

Me: "Norah's Café. We found new evidence."

Dewey: "Oh, I, uh…I just realized that I have a…uh…dentist appointment right now that I am late for. Gotta go."

And with that he scurried out the door. At that moment Katherine walked in from her office.

Katherine: "Susan, what was that about?"

Me: "Dewey turned down a job to take photos and ran out the door!"

Katherine: "He actually turned down a job?"

My thoughts raced until I put it together…

Me: "Ya'll, do you think Dewey is behind this?"

Alex: "Hmm! You know, I have a rabbit lady friend who may be able to help."

Katherine: "A rabbit? How could she help?"

Alex: "Well, I could have her come over to Norah's and she can see where the hole leads. Boom! We find our culprit. I am not traipsing through a dirty hole!"

I liked this idea, but was beginning to be skeptical of everybird and every creature at this point.

Me: "Good idea Alex, but is your friend trustworthy? What if a rabbit stole the seed?"

Alex: "Honey, that is not her thing. Her family owns the Old Cottontail Mill. She does not resort to stealing food or even digging her own tunnels. Her name is Evelyn, by the way."

Me: "I say call her up and let's get this case solved."

We made arrangements with Alex's rabbit friend to meet at some point to investigate at Norah's Café. Could Dewey really be behind this? I needed proof before accusing Dewey. All residents of our great town deserve that, no matter how annoying they may be.

FOOD DRIVE TONIGHT FOR NORAH'S CAFE

LEK PERFORMANCE TICKET GIVEAWAY

by Susan Towhee - Published June 12, 2022 in the Restful Roost Observer

Join your fellow Restful Roosters tonight at the community center at 7 p.m. to support local business owner Norah Nuthatch by bringing a seed donation. Any spare seed you can offer will be appreciated! As reported earlier in the Observer, Nuthatch's store, Norah's Café, was burglarized and inventory depleted. Norah needs our help to re-open! Jed's Pub, owned and operated by Jed Jaeger, has offered to supply free beer and snacks to those who bring a donation or help to pack up and deliver goods to Norah's.

A ticket for the free beer and snacks will be provided at the community center when you make your donation. Be sure to write your name on the ticket stub as one lucky winner will receive two free tickets to the June 14th Spectacular Lek Performance show with appearances by Greater Sage, Gunnison, and Sharp Tailed Grouses. There will also be a special appearance by Greater & Lesser Prairie-Chickens. The winner will be drawn at a later date. Thanks to Charlene Chickadee for organizing the donation event and ticket giveaway. Thanks also to Jed for the beer and snacks!

See you all there tonight!

As soon as I woke I called Alex to make sure things were still set to meet at Norah's Café with his rabbit friend. Things were still a go so I made sure my mate Adam knew to pack up and bring some seed to the community center tonight. I was looking forward to helping Norah get back on her feet and I was ready for a pint or two with my fellow Roosters. First, I had to attend the weekly book club meeting at the library.

When I arrived at the library I found Norah Nuthatch, Marilyn Dove, Goldy Goldfinch, Mary Robin, Charlene Chickadee, and the town librarian, Thea Bobwhite, already there. That week's book was *To Kill a Mockingbird.* As usual, we spent more time catching up and discussing the latest news than about the book.

Thea: "Glad you could make it, Susan!"

Me: "I wouldn't miss a book club session! No matter what new crime has occurred!"

Marilyn: "We were just telling Norah that we will all be there tonight to provide assistance! Norah, I speak for Mayor Andrew when I say we are thinking about you and hope the chief catches the thief soon."

Goldy: "Don't hold your breath on that!"

Marilyn: "What do you mean?"

Charlene: "Marilyn! The police chief is washed up! He doesn't know what he is doing anymore. You really need to talk to the Mayor and tell him the town is getting agitated. We need a change!"

Norah: "Charlene is right. Ever since the theft, I have received no follow ups and no assurances that the police are on top of this."

Mary: "I do agree that a change is needed within the police department. I am afraid that change may come to a new mayor as well if we see crime continue to occur throughout the town."

Marilyn: "I can't believe my own friends are ganging up on me like this! I may have a fainting attack! I need to get away from you all!"

Marilyn flew out the library as her feathers whistled.

Goldy: "Geez, clutch your pearls lady! We didn't say a bad thing about Andrew."

Mary: "Well, I did mention a change in a mayor may be coming. I meant it, too."

Me: "Mary, we all appreciate your fierce devotion to this town! Maybe you should run for mayor!"

All ladies cooed their approval to that suggestion.

Mary: "No, I am not interested. You couldn't pay me to hold public office. I will happily stick to medicine."

Thea then tried to steer the discussion back to the book.

Thea: "Enough politics! Let's focus on the book! Now, who all read the book and who all just watched the movie?"

I arrived early at the community center later that day so I could help Charlene Chickadee with the set up.

Charlene: "Thank you so much for the help, Susan! I am expecting a large crowd especially since Jed is offering free beer! I really need to get an assistant soon."

Me: "No problem! I hope I can gather extra intel at the event."

Charlene: "Sometimes I wonder why we even have a police department when you and other town citizens end up investigating and solving all of the crimes around here!"

Me: "Yea, Chief Finch has lost a bit of his edge lately that is for sure."

Charlene: "Maybe we should start a campaign for the mayor to appoint someone new as chief. Or a campaign for a new mayor! All Andrew seems to do is golf. He hardly ever checks in on the center. Mary was right, a change is needed."

Me: "That is something to think about. Maybe you can submit an opinion letter to the paper on it."

Charlene: "I will consider it. Let's see how he does with this newest crime."

At that moment a loud CAW scream was heard in the community center. We turned to see Alex Crow flying towards us.

Alex: "OMG! I am so glad I found you Susan! The thief has struck again and the victim is ME! CAW!"

Me: "Ok, slow down and tell me what happened."

Charlene: "Wait, did you call the chief to report it?"

Alex: "Why waste my time with him!? I need to go to the Feds with this story. So, I was putting the trash out behind my salon and I noticed ALL of the bags of trash in my special feathers only dumpster were GONE."

Me: "Wow! Yes, that is a federal crime and it needs to be reported asap. I think I still have the number for the FBI that were here for the cowbird disaster."

In case you are wondering why this is such a big deal, I will tell you. Bird feather collection is a big no no in the bird world. We have to securely store and dispose of discarded feathers. Selling feathers is an illegal activity. Restful Roost has drop off boxes to deposit feathers and Alex's nail salon has a special dumpster he has to put them in. Once a month a collection company stops by to pick it all up. Humans love birds so much that they made it illegal in the human world as well. This is all detailed in the human government document called the Migratory Bird Treaty Act. I recommend giving that a good reading.

Alex: "Give me the number Susan and I will call the Feds now, but please alert everybird in town to be on the lookout. Also tell them to protect their coverts and primaries!"

Charlene: "I will print and post something now for the community board so everybird sees it tonight."

Me: "Good idea! I will call the chief to report it as well."

Chief Finch: "Report what to the chief, Susan?"

Chief Finch surprised us as he flew into the center. I filled him in.

Me: "Well chief, you just missed Alex Crow. He said his feather dumpster was raided and all feathers are gone. He is calling the Feds now to report it. I think the thief has upped his game."

Chief Finch: "Oh lordy, just what I need is for the Feds to be back in town. Look, who knows if the thief is the same one. I mean, seeds and feathers? That doesn't make sense."

Me: "Well our office is missing pencils and who knows what else if we start looking. Maybe other residents are missing items too but they just don't know it yet."

Chief Finch: "I better head over to Preen and dust for featherprints. Tell Jed to save me a beer for later."

At that time birds started flying in with their donations. Norah greeted each bird. She was joined by a late arriving Mayor Dove. Norah and the mayor thanked each bird as they gave out a ticket for the free beer and snacks at Jed's Pub. Alex mentioned that after the event we would head back to the café to meet up with his rabbit friend for more sleuthing. I mingled and interrogated as many birds as I could. I also heard the now rampant gossip about the feather theft. I heard everything from "it's the Victorian hats with feathers in them making a comeback" to "I bet a bird is selling them to Montana fly fishermen for top dollar." The case needed to be solved soon to prevent mass hysteria.

After the donation event and after a couple of beers at Jed's I arrived at Norah's Café with Alex and Norah already waiting. I met a lovely female Eastern Cottontail rabbit. This was Alex's friend Evelyn Cottontail. After a quick introduction she said she wanted to get right to the task. She said she would report back where the trail led.

After 5 minutes or so she returned with quite a story.

Evelyn: "Whoever did this is quite a hoarder! I found tons of seeds, office supplies, feathers, cans, broken glass, you name it!"

Office supplies! I immediately thought of Dewey!

Alex: "Caw! Excuse me, did you say feathers? OMG, what if those are my missing feathers? This thief is *sooo* going to prison. I need to contact the Feds with an update."

I brought up my concerns about Dewey.

Me: "Could it be a chipmunk?"

Evelyn: "Sure, it could be. Rats and squirrels hoard as well, so it could be any local animal."

Alex: "Well my money is on Dewey as the thief! Sounds

like he has been acting real cagey lately. Plus, chipmunks are annoying. I bet he wants to sell the feathers on the black market. No wonder he doesn't want to work lately. He is too busy making money elsewhere."

Norah: "Where exactly was the hoard?"

Evelyn: "From what I can tell it is two blocks over under the back patio at the human Smith house."

Norah: "Oh I know the place! They always have tasty suet cakes available and a nice clean birdbath."

Alex: "Yass I know the place! There are two gorgeous cherry trees in the backyard!"

Evelyn: "What I did notice were a lot of tunnels dug at the hoard stash. Rocks were falling in and mud was everywhere, so I hope the Smiths have insurance on their patio. Whatever is causing this has to be ruining their property!"

Me: "That is another reason to catch this culprit! The Smiths may stop feeding the birds if they think a rodent is stealing all of their seeds and causing havoc! We should tell the chief and see if he can investigate further at the hoard site. Maybe search for hair or other clues to pinpoint exactly what species is responsible. No matter how annoying, we don't place blame on a creature. Innocent until proven guilty and all."

As expected, when I notified the chief, he said he needed more evidence. He even refused to search the hole or speak with Evelyn about what she saw. Since he was not willing to do his job, this meant we had to do something. It was decided that Norah, Alex, and I would fly over to the Smith backyard and have an old fashioned stakeout!

We arrived around 10 p.m. loaded with binoculars, snacks, and water. We got cozy in one of the cherry trees. Who knew how long this would take!

Norah reminisced about the fundraiser earlier that night.

Norah: "I can't believe the generosity of the birds in this town!"

Me: "We all stick together! With the success of tonight you should be able to open soon."

Alex: "And we all know there are plenty of places to get fresh bird seed around town, I mean, look at this yard! I see hot pepper suet, cupcakes with cranberries, sunflower seed stations, mealworms, you name it, but your café is a social meeting place with comfy seats and great coffee. Plus, reliable WIFI!"

Me: "Alex is right. Your café is special and it means something to Restful Roost."

Norah: "I appreciate you two! Plus, Jed said he can't keep up with feeding the extra customers."

Alex: "Hopefully this case will be resolved tonight so we can rest easy without a sick klepto in our midst."

After idle chit chat for an hour or so we heard the back door open at the Smith residence. The couple brought out a metallic rectangular box and set it near the patio.

Alex: "What on earth is that contraption?"

I racked my brain until I remembered.

Me: "Oh my! I think I know what that is. I read about it once at college. Let me fly down to get a better look."

Alex: "Be careful! Setting up a weird device late at night spells trouble. Maybe we can't trust humans!"

Once the Smiths went back inside I flew over to check out the strange box. Upon review I was right. I had read about this. I knew exactly what it was and I also knew not to get any closer. I flew back up to our stakeout position.

Me: "I knew it! It is a trap! It is for catching nuisance animals. There is peanut butter smeared at the end of it inside the cage. Once an animal enters the trap the lid closes and traps them!"

Norah: "Oh my! The Smiths must mean business with that thing."

Alex: "Yes, I mean look at the damage to their yard! Holes everywhere and piles of rocks by the patio. I mean we birds are messy too, what with the occasional poop releasing when we take off, but this is territory damage on a large scale."

Me: "Thanks for the visual Alex. I for one, aim my poops at the ground and not on objects!"

Alex: "Shh! I hear something!"

In the corner of the yard we saw a small movement near a hole.

Norah: "The creature must have burrowed in towards the cache."

Me: "Let's hope it re-appears in another hole on the way out so we can ID it. Thankfully the moon is helping with natural lightning."

Within five minutes we saw the perp. None other than Dewey Chipmunk appeared in a hole right in front of us!

Quiet gasps arose from us as we saw Dewey approach the cage.

Norah: "Should we warn him?"

Alex: "Uh, honey, do you remember he almost tanked your business? I say let's see what happens."

Me: "I read that the traps are mostly for catch and release so I don't expect anything nefarious will happen to him at the hands of the Smiths."

At that time we saw the tail of Dewey disappear into the cage and shortly later a clang noise as the lid fell shut.

There was silence in the tree as we watched the Smiths exit the back door and approach the cage.

Mr. Smith approached the cage and peered in.

Mr. Smith: "We got the little bastard!"

The Smiths went back in the house and returned with a towel and a box. They draped the towel over the cage and put the cage in a box and off they went with Dewey Chipmunk.

NORAH'S CAFE THIEF CAUGHT

DEWEY CHIPMUNK REMAINS AT LARGE

RESIDENTS RALLY FOR CAFE SEED DRIVE

by Susan Towhee - Published June 13, 2022 in the
Restful Roost Observer

Major developments occurred overnight in the recent theft case at Norah's Café. Eyewitnesses were able to determine that Restful Roost resident Dewey Chipmunk was responsible for the theft of seed at the café, office supply theft at his place of work (the malefactor worked as a photographer at the Restful Roost Observer), and feather theft from Alex Crows' beauty salon Preen. Thanks to a local citizen (who wishes to remain anonymous) large caches of seeds, office supplies, feathers, and random trash were found in burrows created by Dewey. The citizen was able to trace the burrows by entering a hole located in the basement of Norah's Café and following it to a burrow under the property of a local human couple named the Smiths.

Police and the FBI have been unable to locate Dewey as he was caught, trapped, and relocated by the Smiths late last night. Dewey's main cache was located in the backyard of the Smith property. "His burrowing was causing a foundation problem at the home of the Smiths. It seems as if they took the matter into their own hands and also helped us out a bit by catching the perp and relocating him. Among the stash we found all of Norah Nuthatch's winter supply, illegal storing of feathers, and a large amount of pencils which are property of the local newspaper. If anybird is missing items please contact the police. As soon as we are done clearing the cache we can determine if your item is among the stolen goods," said Chief Joe E. Finch.

Among the cache was a large collection of feathers. The feathers were stolen earlier in the week at the Preen salon. Owner Alex Crow had a message for Dewey. "If the FBI does not find you, rest assured I will," said Crow. Since feather possession is a federal crime, this case has been transferred to the local FBI field office.

The police want the public to know that if anybird sees Dewey, is contacted by him, or has any other information, to please call the police department at 55-TWEET.

In positive news, a food drive held at the Restful Roost Community Center proved a great success in replenishing stock for Norah's Café. "I just wanted to help in some way. If my business was ransacked by a crazy rat [sic] I know others in town would help me as well," said pub owner Jed Jaeger, who offered free snacks and drinks for donations. Norah Nuthatch was very appreciative of the support and is confident her business will get back to normal within weeks. "I am still upset that Dewey was taken in such a horrible way, but we do need law and order here and no one's personal property should be violated. I would like to personally thank all residents of Restful Roost who participated in the seed drive last night. Since most of my cache was located and will be returned to me, I want to welcome everybird back to the café for a complimentary coffee and seed tray," said Nuthatch.

So what happened to Dewey Chipmunk? Where was he taken? Why was he stealing everything he could? What was he planning to do with all of those feathers? Katherine Heron would also like to know why he stole all of her damn pencils.

Just another day in Restful Roost.

~ 3 ~

FERAL FELINE

The Story (as I remember it)...

The time was about 11 p.m. and my mate Adam and I had just left the Restful Roost Community Center after an amazing concert by the great Cherry Chat. When I hear "Can't Fly Anymore," that really takes me back to high school! We decided to stop by Jed's Pub for a quick bourbon and cigar. While there, Jed's police scanner came to life while he screamed about yet another crime. Jed had the scanner installed to keep up with local mischief. Was he just interested in what was happening or was he planning a run for mayor soon? Town residents have been wanting a new police chief appointed for some time now and only the mayor could appoint one. Local chatter was that Jed was being considered as a possible mayoral candidate. The police scanner indicated an ANM code (Animal Complaint), then shortly after an ASL (Assault), finally a DB code was announced. That one stands for Dead Body, ladies and gentlebirds! The location was the town square which meant only a short fly away to investigate. Thankfully I was only one bourbon drink in!

I arrived at a gruesome scene. Multiple dead birds lie on the ground next to the town square fountain. Police Chief Joe E. Finch, town doctor Mary Robin, and town nurse Simon Sparrow were on the scene.

Me: "Evening Chief, what on earth happened here?"

Chief Finch: "Well, little lady, it looks like a mass murder. We are still investigating what they were doing here, what birds they are, and what creature is responsible."

Mary Robin approached us with her gloves on her wings and a solemn expression.

Mary: "These are Tennessee Warblers and most likely were on fall migration. This region is a common path for them. I found hairs that we will analyze. I have already sent Simon to the lab to get started, but my hunch is a cat did this."

Chief Finch: "Oh, no! We don't have murderous cats here. Let's not rush to judgment. And Susan, you better not report that."

Me: "Chief, I only report the facts!"

At that moment a loud coo was heard behind us. The town mayor, Andrew Dove, had arrived and he was very much inebriated. Should I report that? It was a fact...

Mayor Dove: "I heard you about a cat and I say no! I bet that no good Jaeger did this!"

Mary: "The Jaeger? You mean Jed? You must be crazy!"

Me: "He had nothing to do with this, Mr. Mayor. I was at his pub when the crime happened and he never left my sight."

By this time a crowd had appeared and all most likely heard the mayor's rantings about Jed being the murderer.

Chief Finch: "I will be the one investigating all angles here. Now everybird needs to leave so we can wrap this crime scene up."

I hung around for a bit to check if anything suspicious was happening, but whoever had done this was long gone. For the town's sake I hoped the chief would find this killer and find it fast!

MIGRATING BIRDS MURDERED

SUSPECT AT LARGE

by Susan Towhee - Published September 16, 2022
in the Restful Roost Observer

Three dead birds were found near the town square fountain last night, all murdered.

According to town doctor Mary Robin, the birds were identified as migrating Tennessee Warblers. Hairs were also found at the scene which her lab is currently testing.

Police Chief Joe E. Finch told the paper that they

have no suspects but will investigate all avenues. If the public has any information please call the police department at 55-TWEET.

Stay vigilant Restful Roost!

For me, the next day began with our weekly book club meeting at the library. All the usual members were there: Norah Nuthatch, Goldy Goldfinch, Mary Robin, Charlene Chickadee, and town librarian Thea Bobwhite. All were present except for Marilyn Dove, the mayor's wife. She had been avoiding the club ever since we cast doubts on her husband's ability to do his job. Rumors were that she was so distraught that she wanted Andrew to quit and for them both to move to Florida.

Thea: "Thank you all for being on time today. As you all know the book this week is *The Bald Eagle* by Jack E. Davis. Before we discuss, I would like us to hold a moment of silence for the lives lost last night."

All agreed and held the moment. Mary Robin quietly broke the news to us.

Mary: "It was a cat."

Gasps arose from the group!

Me: "You got the results back already?"

Mary: "Yes, we had similar hairs already on file that we quickly matched up to the ones we found last night. It is a local cat."

Goldy: "This has to be the lead story tomorrow Susan!

Rumors are spreading that the chief wants to place blame on Jed!"

Me: "Yes, the mayor started that one. Believe me, if Marilyn was here I would give her an earful about her husband's behavior last night. He was rip roaring drunk!"

Charlene: "Any reasonable citizen knows that Jed wouldn't do such a thing. It has to be a human's pet cat on the prowl."

Norah: "If only they would keep their cats inside! Don't humans know it is harmful to the cat to let it roam outside? Coyote sightings are still a thing around here!"

Mary: "Jed will lose it if he finds out that no good police chief is accusing him. I really hope Jed decides to run for mayor!"

Thea tried to get the conversation back to the book discussion.

Thea: "He would have my vote! He can also use the library as a meeting place. Now, let's get to discussing bald eagles!"

After a rousing discussion on the bald eagle book (by the way, did you know that the bird is not officially recognized as our national bird by humans!?) I decided to grab lunch at Jed's Pub. I also wanted to see just how upset he was about the recent rumor mill. When I entered I sat at an open seat at the bar (a very empty bar) near where Jed was drying dishes.

Jed: "Hey Susan, whatta ya want to eat?"

Me: "I'll take a medium worm sandwich. Hear any more news about the crime last night?"

Jed: "Only that the whole town thinks I am a murderer. Look around, no one is here today!"

Me: "It was a pretty twisted murder! Give birds time to process. Everybird knows you didn't do it. Hell, half the town was crammed in here last night after the concert! They all saw you here."

Jed: "I can't wait until we get new police leadership in town."

Me: "How about those other rumors about you running for mayor? Then you can appoint your own police chief."

Jed: "Gotta say I am thinking more and more on it. Someone else with more experience will probably decide to run."

Me: "Thea said you can use the library as a volunteer meeting place."

Jed: "She really said that? Guess that is one town resident who doesn't think I murder other birds."

Me: "The entire book group knows you are innocent. Stop being dramatic."

Jed: "Fine. One worm sandwich coming up. On the house, too. Thanks for stopping by."

I ate in silence and alone. Hopefully the headline in the paper tomorrow about a cat being responsible will calm birds down and Jed's customers will return. We also needed to get this cat identified and monitored!

LOCAL FELINE RESPONSIBLE FOR BIRD DEATHS

by Susan Towhee - Published September 17, 2022
in the Restful Roost Observer

Town doctor Mary Robin confirmed to the Restful Roost that the hairs found at the crime scene are those belonging to a feline. In fact, the feline is a local cat or at least one that has been in the area recently. Hairs found at the scene were compared to ones collected at a previous scene.

"I just like to tag and bag any weird things I see in the area. You never know when it will help with future cases. This specific blond cat hair belongs to a species called Persian. I think it is safe to say that this cat was responsible for the murders. With the hair found at the scene and wounds similar to cat batting I have no other conclusion," said Robin.

The Restful Roost reached out to Police Chief Joe E. Finch for comment but has not heard back.

If anybird sees a Persian cat roaming the Foliage Forest or the town limits please call the police department at 55-TWEET.

Stay vigilant Restful Roost!

Back at the Restful Roost office the next day, my editor, Katherine Heron, and I spent the time researching cats and any back reports or claims of a Persian cat sighting. After ordering in take out and tired of perching around reading files, Katherine suggested we fly by popular bird feeder locations humans had set up near our town to see if we could locate evidence of cats. I called my mate Adam to inform him I would be late coming home.

Katherine: "If the cat attacked once then it will probably do it again. We might catch it in the act!"

Me: "Yes, especially with so many migrations happening right now. It will be a field day for a cat when he finds tired birds hanging around."

Two hours of flying around (and after stopping by dozens of bird feeder locations) we decided to rest at a pine tree near the human street called Riverside Drive.

Katherine: "Well this is useless! Have any more ideas?"

Me: "No, but what is that smell?"

Katherine: "Ew, who smelt it dealt it."

Me: "Stop it. Nothing I create smells that horrid!"

Katherine: "Oh gross there is a big pile of poo down below."

Me: "Wait, is that what I think it is?"

Katherine: "If poo, then yes."

Me: "No! Cat scat! Look at the sausage shape! I am flying down for a closer look."

Katherine: "Be careful! Oh hell, I am coming with you."

We flew down to investigate. Mindful that the cat may still be around (the feces was still steaming!) we watched each other's wings.

Me: "I see a hair Katherine! Snag it!"

Katherine: "Why do I have to? You identified it!"

Me: "Ugh, ok, I am only doing this to help close this case!"

I very carefully used my toe to snag a hair. So nasty! I then decided to fly straight to the health clinic so Mary Robin could test it. Katherine flew to the police department to alert the chief. We decided to meet back up at Jed's Pub for a late dinner and drink to congratulate ourselves.

Simon: "What are you doing here at this hour? Has something happened?"

Me: "Oh, you bet it has! I guess Mary has the night off. Katherine and I found a hair that appears to match the one Mary described at the crime scene."

Simon: "Let me take a look!"

Me: "Sorry it has a bad smell on it. Please use two sets of gloves. Also, where is the washroom? I need a full foot bath."

Simon: "In the back on the left. Where did you get this?"

Me: "Trust me, you don't want to know the exact location, but we retrieved it at a human residence on Riverside Drive."

Simon: "Yikes, that is the location on the bag for the other hair we compared the crime scene hair to."

Me: "I was hoping it would be a match. Katherine has alerted Chief Finch. Please let me know as soon as you or Mary have details."

After cleaning up (three thorough cleanings!) I flew over to Jed's Pub to meet with Katherine.

When I arrived at the pub I found a chaotic scene. Police Chief Finch was there along with half the town population. I know Jed needed more business, but this did not look promising. I located Katherine to see what was up and she alerted me to quite the news flash.

Katherine: "You won't believe this Susan! Chief Finch arrested Jed for the bird murders!

Me: "Say what!? But we found evidence pointing directly to a neighborhood cat!"

Katherine: "I tried to tell the chief that, but he insisted Jed was behind it. He has already taken him to the jail and is back 'gathering evidence' he says. He also said he has no use for that 'lady bird doctor and her science nonsense' and that he knows how to run an investigation."

Me: "Oh brother. Simon said he will inform us as soon as they have run their tests. Hopefully in time for Jed to be released from jail! I am flying back to the paper to write up this story."

And with that I flew back to the paper to await news on the cat hairs.

Back at the paper I was alerted to more breaking news. Town architect Vincent Vulture was waiting at the office doors as I approached.

Me: "Hey Vincent! We aren't really open right now, but

I was about to write up the headline for tomorrow's paper. How can I help you?"

Vincent: "Susan, I just wanted you to know that I have posted bail for Jed. I was at the pub after the concert when the murders occurred and I know he wasn't responsible. Besides, I know what it is like to be an outcast like Jed. I know some birds in town don't like vultures."

Me: "What a great gesture Vincent! And I do know what you mean, unfortunately. As for me I am grateful you are a resident of this town and I am especially grateful for the cleanups you and your families do to keep this town clean. Maybe a future writeup about the health benefits you offer is in order."

Vincent: "That won't be necessary. I just wanted to make sure you were aware Jed's bail will be posted and he should be released in the morning."

As soon as Vincent flew away, Mary Robin flew in.

Mary: "Susan, was that Vincent Vulture I saw?"

Me: "Yes, Mary it was. He said he posted bail for Jed and he will be released tomorrow."

Mary: "Well that is great to hear! Especially because he had nothing to do with it! I swear the chief has completely lost it! I told him to wait until he made an arrest because I was analyzing the hairs you brought to the clinic. He refused to listen to me!"

Me: "I heard he did not believe in the 'little lady bird science nonsense' or something like that."

Mary: "The nerve! Well I found that the hairs do match."

Me: "Perfect. Now, the issue is, since the chief is useless, how is Restful Roost going to deal with the cat?"

JAEGER ARRESTED IN BIRD MURDER CASE

BAIL PAID; JAEGER RELEASED

LOCAL FELINE LINKED TO CRIME

by Susan Towhee - Published September 18, 2022 in the Restful Roost Observer

Restful Roost Police Chief Joe E. Finch arrested local businessbird Jed Jaeger last night at Jed's business establishment, Jed's Pub. Chief Finch said he is confident Jed is the murderer of the migrating Tennessee Warblers found earlier this week. "The Jaeger is a known predator of smaller birds, the victims were found right outside his pub near the town square, and he has been very hostile to the local police," said Finch.

Town citizens aren't quite buying the chief's reasoning on this matter. At the time of the crime Jed was pouring drinks for a packed crowd after the Cherry Chat concert on September 15. Hairs found at the scene belong to a cat. Jed has witnesses to vouch for his whereabouts, no feathers belonging to him were found at the scene, and Jed is a respected local leader. Local businessbird Vincent Vulture agreed. He posted bail last night and Jed will be released from custody this morning.

Adding to the confusion about the arrest is town doctor Mary Robin. Last night Restful Roost editor Katherine Heron and myself were able to locate further cat hair evidence from a nearby human home. (The residence was at 666 Riverside Dr. Please avoid this area!) Hairs were immediately flown to the health clinic where Mary Robin identified them as the same hairs found at the murder site. "There is no doubt in my mind that a cat is responsible. Science does not lie," said Robin. Police Chief Finch would not comment on the hair discovery nor would he comment on the release of Jed.

Stay tuned for further developments!

After a lazy morning at the paper, I decided to fly to Jed's Pub to see how he was doing. On the door was a note stating that the pub was closed for the day. I assumed Jed just needed to rest up from being up all night. Also, he needed a bit of privacy. I grabbed a couple of sandwiches to go from Norah's Cafe and brought them back for Katherine and I for lunch. After eating and filing more stories the paper's police scanner awoke with yet another call of DB. Dead body! This was also at the town square. Katherine and I grabbed our pen and papers and off we flew.

When we arrived, the scene was not as we expected. No migrating or local birds were found at the scene. Instead we found the corpse of a Persian Cat!

I approached Mary who was already on the scene and bagging evidence.

Me: "Mary, is this the cat I think it is?"

Mary: "I will have to do some tests, but my gut says yes."

Katherine: "Where is Chief Finch?"

Mary: "Who knows! As soon as I arrived he said he had 'things' to do."

Katherine: "Embarrassed about being wrong most likely."

Me: "I hate to see murder in any species, but this will make the town safer."

After a few more minutes at the scene I decided to fly back to the office to file my report. Before I left, and I could have been mistaken, I swear I saw Jed watching the scene from the pub's roof.

DEAD FELINE FOUND IN TOWN SQUARE

HAIRS LINK FELINE TO BIRD MURDERS

by Susan Towhee - Published September 19, 2022
in the Restful Roost Observer

Yesterday afternoon a deceased Persian cat was found near the town square fountain. No witnesses saw the death occur.

Town doctor Mary Robin has concluded that hairs found on the cat match the hairs from the migrating bird murder case.

Police Chief Joe E. Finch, while initially on the scene, could not be reached for comment.

While the migrating bird case appears to be solved, authorities still need information on what or who may have killed the cat. Please call the police department at 55-TWEET if you have any information.

So what happened to the cat? Poison? A coyote?

Why was the police chief so reluctant to listen to Mary Robin?

Did the chief and the mayor have a vendetta against Jed?

Were they afraid for their jobs?

Seems they should be afraid as this latest crime had the town shook. Citizens are also angry at the handling of the arrest of Jed.

As for Jed, the whole episode seems to have motivated him. He has announced that he will start a mayoral exploration committee with a meeting soon at the community center. He will also start a new non profit: Cat Free Restful Roost (CFRR). I was honored to join him as a founding member.

Just another day in Restful Roost.

~ 4 ~

A HOPPY HAUNTING

The Story (as I remember it)....

It was nearing 11 p.m. and my mate (Adam) and I were enjoying a quiet night at home watching my favorite horror movie, the remake of *House on Haunted Hill*. Well, I should say I was watching it as Adam had fallen asleep an hour ago. Just as the credits were rolling and my bourbon glass emptied, the police scanner I had installed at my nest blared an AIR police code at the nearby Old Gavin Mill. AIR? That was an aircraft incident. What in the world? This was near Halloween, of course. Perhaps misguided youth playing a prank. Regardless, I had to find out for myself. Off I flew to investigate.

I arrived to find Chad Cardinal talking with Police Chief Joe E. Finch. They were surrounded by a family of rabbits. The Old Cottontail Mill was home to the wealthiest family in Restful Roost. The Cottontail family gained their wealth from running the grist mill and the patriarch was none other than the famous movie actor Hopper Cottontail. He is very elusive and we all strive to give him his privacy. I searched everywhere in sight, but I could see no downed airplane nor any smoke or fire. I recognized Evelyn Cottontail from our previous work together on a seed theft case. I approached her to see what she knew about this supposed aircraft incident.

Me: "Hey Evelyn! Can I get a quote from you on what happened or any info at all?"

Evelyn: "Hello Susan! Great to see you again! From what I can tell this cardinal was flying by after work and said he saw strange lights."

Me: "Strange lights? Maybe you all had the grist mill lights on?"

"No lassie. Twasn't the mill. Was an outer space being." A booming voice said from behind.

I turned to see none other than Mr. Hopper Cottontail in the fur!

Me: "Oh, sir, what an honor! Say, can you repeat that?"

Hopper: "Sure, that fancy red boy over talking to the chief saw what we see this time of the year every year. Multicolored lights, odd noises, very weird smells, you name it and it happens here at the mill."

Police Chief Finch and Chad approached.

Chief Finch: "Mr. Cottontail, sir, it is great to meet you!"

Hooper: "And I should say it is not quite an honor to meet you. I have read up on you and your no good policing. Why, you should be ashamed. And I heard you talking to this fine young red lad. You think he is crazy and only saw fireflies. Bah! He saw what we see here every Halloween! This place is haunted I tell you!"

Chief Finch turned so red you would think he was a Purple Finch!

Chad: "I know what I saw! It was a craft with changing lights. Quite scary!"

Hopper: "It can be, but we learn to live with it."

Me: "Chad, what are you doing here at this time of night?"

Chief Finch: "That is what I would like to know as well. Meeting a lady friend here for a late night rendezvous? Smoking drugs? Hitting the booze?"

Chad: "Of course not. I was working late with Vincent, and was on my way home. We just finished building the new Inn and we were finalizing things to be ready for the grand opening tomorrow night. He will tell you I was with him!"

Chief Finch: "You bet I will check with him. I say this is all Halloween hysteria and you all must be on drugs to see spooky lights at night all the time. Must be some weird Hollywood acid you get from this acting clown."

Hopper: "I am a gentlebird, but if you do not leave my property right now I will throw you in my grist mill and grind your feathers and bones to a fine dust."

Chief Finch: "I should arrest you for threatening an officer of the law!"

Me: "Chief, maybe you should head over to the Inn and find Vincent before he leaves for the night. You can corroborate Chad's story."

Chief Finch: "Quite right. You all better not leave town."

Off the chief flew in a rush and in the wrong direction no less.

Hopper: "Well I guess I put my foot in my mouth. Hope I didn't make it too bad for you my young red friend."

Chad: "It's okay. I know what I saw. I can provide a sketch for the paper."

Me: "Thanks Chad! And don't worry Mr. Cottontail, you said what we all wanted to say to the chief. Now, can I get some more information on what else goes on here at the mill? It sounds like quite a story."

Evelyn: "How about you both come in for some hot cocoa and we can share with you all we know."

After two hours of tantalizing tales of hauntings and visitations I left to write up quite a tale just in time for Halloween.

STRANGE LIGHTS REPORTED AT MILL

EXCLUSIVE INTERVIEW:
HOPPER COTTONTAIL ON MILL HAUNTINGS

THE RAVENS CONCERT TONIGHT

NEW INN GRAND OPENING TONIGHT

by Susan Towhee - Published October 31, 2022 in
the Restful Roost Observer

It is certainly Halloween here in Restful Roost! Late last night Police Chief Joe E. Finch was called out to the nearby Old Cottontail Mill to investigate a report of strange lights. Local construction worker Chad Cardinal was on his way home from work when he spotted bright lights flashing on and off right above the mill. "I know what I saw. It wasn't lightning bugs or swamp gas. These were unidentified flying objects," said Cardinal.

Chief Finch was not amused by the late night call. "These young hooligans think they know everything. There is no such thing as UFOs. Most likely a prank since it is Halloween time and all," said Finch.

Last night's UFO's or UAP's (Unidentified Aerial Phenomenon, as they are now called) were also spotted by various members of the Eastern Cottontail rabbit family who live on site at the mill. In an exclusive interview, famed actor and mill owner Hopper Cottontail shared with me that the lights and other paranormal activity are common near the mill.

Hopper Cottontail: "These sightings are nothing new. Every Halloween Eve and Halloween we are visited here. Each time is something new. Could be flashing lights, a visitation from a non Earth being, odd smells, you name it."

Susan Towhee: "We can get into specifics in a

minute, but why is this the first time this activity has been reported?"

Hopper Cottontail: "Well, we rabbits are very secretive. If these events became public knowledge we may be labeled as kooks. It also appears that the activity is only occurring right at our mill. The young red lad just happened to be there at the right time and place."

Susan Towhee: "Why do you think your mill attracts such activity?"

Hopper Cottontail: "Back in the 1800's there was a horrible incident on site. You see, the mill is located right next to train tracks and at the time there was a very busy train stop right across from the mill. In 1868, while the train was stopped to load and unload passengers an explosion occurred. My great great grandfather died. Details are very sketchy as to what happened. Stranger still, his body was never recovered. Eyewitness accounts were very murky. Investigators said it was a planted bomb. The governor at the time even offered a $1000 reward for information. We think that event triggered unrest and the place has been haunted ever since."

Susan Towhee: "That is a horrible crime! Do you think you are being visited by your great great grandfather or the bomber?"

Hopper Cottontail: "Hard to say. We all feel the presence is calming and curious so perhaps it has nothing to do with the incident at all."

Susan Towhee: "What specific occurrences have you and your family witnessed?"

Hopper Cottontail: "Well, one Halloween night we saw a glowing being. It was bright green and it communicated telepathically to us. It told us to be wary of the upcoming rains. We took heed and left town for the week. That same week came the worst flood in the history of Restful Roost. Another Halloween Eve we all were awakened late at night by the most marvelous, fragrant scent of roses. Now, these flowers are not blooming at this time of year so we all went outside to look around. We never could find the source of the smell, but the next morning my granddaughter Evelyn gave birth to 7 beautiful kittens. We think it was a sign of good tidings. There have been other sightings, too, but those are the most memorable."

Susan Towhee: "What wonderful stories and memories. I do agree there is something special going on here."

Hopper Cottontail: "Quite, quite. I want your readers to know that what goes on here is nothing to fear. In fact, your red young lad seems to have been affected in quite a powerful way. I think it has excited his curiosity. And, now that the secret is out, perhaps you and your paper can help my family get to the bottom of what really happened that day in 1868."

Susan Towhee: "It would be my honor to help settle an old Cottontail family mystery. I do thank you for your time discussing this. Please let your visitors know that, if they so choose, the rest of Restful Roost would love a visit!"

Hopper Cottontail: "Oh, I certainly will. Lovely chat and Happy Halloween to you and the whole town."

Popular rock group The Ravens will be performing tonight at the Restful Roost Community Center. For those who imbibe too much tonight and are unable to fly home safely, the local Cottontail rabbit family will be offering complimentary rides home after the show.

For those who want to make a night of it, the brand new Restful Roost Inn will have its grand opening immediately after the concert with free appetizers and drinks. Owner Peter Woodpecker is also offering 50% off room rates tonight. "I hope the discount entices birds to check out my new hotel and see what a wonderful job architect Vincent Vulture has done with the place. I am especially proud of the elegant wine tasting room which is stocked with only the best local wines," said Woodpecker.

Restful Roost: keep your eyes to the sky!

The town was abuzz with the Old Cottontail Mill lights

story. My editor, Katherine Heron, gave me the green light to proceed with an investigation of the 1868 train explosion. While in the office we discussed the concert that night, whether we needed to hire a new photographer or just take photos ourselves, and how the paper could help with the new non profit CFRR (Cat Free Restful Roost) which would hold its first meeting next month.

Me: "Well I plan on enjoying the night and taking up Peter Woodpecker on his offer of 50% off a room. Nothing like a fancy hotel with room service! Will you be attending the show Katherine?"

Katherine: "Hell yes. Front row seats! I hope they do a meet and greet after the show! Feel free to take the next 2 days off to rest. That is, unless we have more UFO sightings."

Me: "Thanks for that! Time for lunch! Jed's special worm sandwiches?"

Katherine: "You bet! Let's go!"

On our way we decided to take a quick detour and fly to the Old Cottontail Mill. Katherine wanted to see exactly where the old train station would have been. While investigating the area, I had the thrill of my life! Right in front of us a glowing orb appeared!

Katherine: "Susan, please tell me you see this, too!"

Me: "Yes, I can't take my peepers off of it. Can you feel that?"

Katherine: "You mean the feeling of weightlessness? Yes, I feel it."

Me: "Unbelievable!"

And just like that, the orb disappeared.

Me: "That looked just like what reports of orbs at Skinwalker Ranch in Utah looked like."

Katherine: "Well our orb had a pleasant feeling, not a menacing one. I feel like I just had a four hour spa treatment and a two hour nap."

Me: "I agree! We gotta go tell the chief about this. It wouldn't surprise me if he arrests Chad on some trumped up charge. He has to know this is real."

So much for thinking the chief would give us a welcoming ear! We explained what we saw and how it made us feel, but the chief wouldn't listen.

Chief Finch: "You ladies have lost it! What were you doing? Smoking hash with that Hopper clown at the mill?"

Katherine: "Smoking hash? What year is it? Look, Susan and I both saw it and wanted you to know. Maybe you should hang out over there some today so that presence over there can remove that stick out of your cloaca."

Chief Finch: "How dare you talk to an officer of the law that way! I am calling the mayor right now and we will have that rag of yours shut down!"

Katherine: "Whatever! Susan, order two cameras from Amazon asap so they arrive in two hours. We need to document this next time it happens."

We left the police department with the chief screaming

at us about saying no to drugs and flew off to Jed's Pub. Katherine approved a lunch time beer to decompress. We found a very crowded and loud pub.

Katherine: "I feel that relaxation we felt at the mill has all evaporated thanks to the stuck in the 1950's chief. What is going on here Susan? This place is packed!"

Me: "I see Chad in the corner with a crowd. Let's check it out."

Chad was talking to about fifty birds all crowded around him. He was recounting his version of what he saw at the mill. The birds yelled out that they had seen things, too. Shouts all around us of:

"Yep, I have seen lights, too!"

"Saw a ghost there once!"

"Bigfoot waved at me!"

Katherine: "Susan Towhee and I just saw a glowing orb!"

Me: "Why have none of you come to the paper about the sightings?"

Murmurs from everybird...

Chad: "Well, Susan, I think it's like this...we were afraid to. You know what birds say about those who see UFOs. They will think we are cuckoo. Like crazy, you know, not like an actual cuckoo."

Me: "I do understand that. Everybird, aren't you all aware that the government is basically now admitting these things are real? Photos and videos exist now! Please feel free to share your story! I know the Cottontail family would appreciate the support!"

More shouts all around us:

"She's right!"

"I will write an op-ed on this!"

"I should write a book!"

"We should do ghost tours!"

Soon the crowd died down and Katherine and I sat at the bar to order our worm sandwiches and a cold Jacka-lope Snowman Stout from Jed.

Me: "Hey Jed, do you believe in UFOs?"

Jed: "Yes, I do, Susan. We are not alone."

Katherine: "Tell that to the chief. He dismissed us as drug users and then said he was going to get the mayor to shut our paper down."

Jed: "He said what!? I swear, he needs to be thrown out of office. It's an embarrassment!"

Me: "So when you are elected the next town mayor, who will you install as police chief?"

Jed: "I am still thinking of a run. These events aren't helping me give the chief another chance, though. I would do a country wide search and interview like crazy. Only the best should represent Restful Roost law enforcement!"

That night we had one of the loudest and craziest con-certs ever to come to Restful Roost! The band announced a meet and greet after the show at the new Restful Roost Inn. If the free food and drinks didn't bring the crowd in to the new hotel, the meet and greet for sure would! The party at the Inn included Pokeberry Punch which made Mary Robin, among others, quite tipsy. Mary proceeded to dance on the tables. Chad Cardinal kept pecking at his reflection in the punch bowl. He wasn't drunk, that was just something he likes to do for fun. Most inebriated of all was our mayor. He made his rounds to everybird in attendance to ask for cash donations for his re-election run.

As fun as the show and after party were, the events later that night would go down as quite memorable in Restful Roost history. At around 1 a.m. the booze ran out. Jed announced a pop up beer garden on the town square and everybird rushed out to get in line.

That is when the incident happened.

As the crowd was partying in the town square a large hush fell on the crowd.

Above us an enormous saucer shaped UFO began a descent on the town square lawn. The silence was deafening as we all waited for what seemed like an hour for something to happen.

As we waited, the chief appeared and promptly fainted as soon as he saw the craft. The rest of us were caught between either fright or excitement.

Then, a noise as a door slowly opened from the craft.

A being exited...a hairy being....or is that fur... wait...it's a rabbit! What is happening here?

The being spoke.

"I am looking for the rabbit they call Hopper."

Whispers, shushes, and "oh my's" circulated around the square.

Hopper Cottontail walked up and approached the being.

Hopper: "I am the one they call Hopper."

Evelyn: "Grandad! What are you doing here?"

Hopper: "What? I may not be able to give rides to birds, but I can still rock and roll at my age!"

The Being: "Please approach the ship."

Hopper: "Would it be okay if you addressed everybird present as to what your plans are this evening?"

The Being: "Of course! I am the rabbit that was taken away in 1868. Rumors were that I was in a train bombing. Well, I almost was. Just as the blast was about to go off I was taken by the creatures who run this spaceship. I was told that my family and I were being monitored and studied. When it appeared my life was in danger they intervened. Eyewitnesses were drained of their memory and my so-called death was questioned for years."

Hopper: "So are you really over one hundred and fifty years old?"

The Being: "No, I was taken at the age I was and my protectors have said I have remained the same age. I do not try to understand their ways."

Hopper: "So what have you been doing this entire time? Why haven't you returned before now?"

The Being: "I have been traveling the universe with my protectors and meeting new species. I have asked if I can return to stay. You see, I have been watching the recent town events and have been quite amused. Also, I would love to know more about my great great grandson. You have made quite a life for yourself!"

Hopper: "Yes, please do! I do wish you will stay so you can tell us more about your protectors and why they have chosen us to watch over."

The Being: "Of course, but, first, perhaps you would like to join me on one last voyage?"

Hopper: "I would be honored and pleased!"

The Being: "Come aboard! And Restful Roost residents, I will see you all soon! I look forward to learning more about each and every one one of you!"

Shouts of "wait!" and "can we see the aliens?" and "do we need to get baptized?" rang from the crowd.

The Being: "More will be explained on my return trip. My protectors are very private and it will be up to them to decide how to present themselves to you all. Good evening and good wishes Restful Roost!"

And with that Hopper and his great great grandfather walked into the ship to be taken on a space journey.

Katherine: "Oh boy, I hope you got photos of that Susan!"

Me: "Yes, close ups, too! I think we need another drink after that. Join me and Adam at the beer garden!"

We walked over to order from Jed.

Me: "Well, Jed, what did you think of that?"

Jed: "Sounds like a bunch of weird new age stuff to me. The spaceship was cool, though."

Adam: "I do hope they both come back safe. And soon! I can't wait to hear stories. It's like our own version of *Star Trek!*"

UFO LANDS IN RESTFUL ROOST

1800'S MISSING RABBIT ON BOARD SHIP

LOCAL ACTOR COTTONTAIL DEPARTS WITH UFO

SOLD OUT PERFORMANCE BY THE RAVENS

NEW INN A HIT WITH TOWN

RESTFUL ROOST GETS "RAVE" REVIEWS

POLICE CHIEF MISSING

by Susan Towhee - Published November 1, 2022
in the Restful Roost Observer

Last night will go down as one of the most memorable ones in Restful Roost history! The town was visited by a UFO which brought back a long ago town resident. As a large crowd gathered in the town square, a large UFO beamed down upon us. Everybird waited to see what would happen and nerves were stretched thin among the crowd. Was this a hostile visitation? Was this a friendly event? Soon we had our answer. A rabbit exited the craft and announced that he was the great great grandfather of local resident and actor Hopper Cottontail. He was returning on friendly terms and only wanted to take his grandson on a space ride!

According to the grandfather, he was saved by the space creatures from a train bombing in the 1800's. Great great grandfather Cottontail also expressed interest in learning more about Restful Roost.

After introductions, the craft left, taking grandfather and grandson with it on a final journey to the unknown. The "protectors" as grandfather Cottontail called them did not present themselves to the crowd. Sometimes too many surprises in one night may be too much for one town to take! The Restful Roost Observer will request an interview with both Hopper and his long lost kin to get more details as soon as possible!

Restful Roost was entertained last night by a loud and rocking sold out show by The Ravens. The band formed in 1975 and has been on a world tour every year since.

The new Restful Roost Inn opened last night and welcomed The Ravens for a post show meet and greet party. Appetizers and cocktails were served at the Inn until all food and drink ran out. "I knew we would have a crowd, but I never expected the turnout we had last night," said Inn owner Peter Woodpecker. "Special thanks to The Ravens for choosing my venue to hang at, all who booked rooms, and to Jed Jaeger who helped serve refreshments when mine ran out," continued Woodpecker.

Lead singer of The Ravens, Edgar Raven, had a four star review for the town. "In our 30 years of touring we have never seen a more rocking crowd. Since this town draws spaceships, oozes paranormal activity, and has a world class hotel, we definitely will be returning. Cheers to Restful Roost," said Raven.

Police Chief Joe E. Finch fled the scene shortly after the arrival of the UFO. His whereabouts are unknown. If anybird has seen or heard from the chief please call the Restful Roost Police Department at 55-TWEET. Calls are being directed to the mayor's office until the chief can be located.

Restful Roost: keep your eyes to the sky!

What a night! Rock and roll and alien visitation! I am glad I took my new camera so I could document the scene. The chief finally woke up from his fainting spell, but as soon as he did, he flew away and no one has seen or heard from him since. I guess his retirement started early. The spacecraft finally returned, but silently and without knowledge of the town. Hopper Cottontail and his great great grandfather were returned safely. Hopper told me he is planning a spoken word play to best present his thoughts and experiences. That was a Halloween to remember!

Just another day in Restful Roost!

~ 5 ~

RED, WHITE, AND BLUE JAY

The Story (as I remember it)....

The morning started off at the weekly book club meeting. That week's book was *Game Change* by Mark Halperin and John Heilemann and it covered the 2008 election. The excitement of the UFO was starting to cease and now the town was talking about the upcoming election for mayor. The usual crew (minus Marilyn Dove) was there: Norah Nuthatch, Goldy Goldfinch, Mary Robin, Charlene Chickadee, and the town librarian, Thea Bobwhite.

Thea: "Ok, who read the book? And who thinks John McCain might have had a chance if he had not picked Palin?"

Me: "Oh, I think Obama had so much momentum nothing would have stopped his win. I do remember being completely confused when I heard she was the veep pick."

Charlene: "I read the book, but can we also discuss Julianne Moore's performance in the movie? So good!"

Goldy: "Can we all discuss the upcoming election? I can't wait to start volunteering!"

Mary: "Well, I certainly won't vote to re-elect Andrew Dove. His behavior has been atrocious lately with all the booze consumption in public. We also need a new chief appointed. Ever since Chief Finch disappeared after the UFO landed we are basically living in a lawless town. Thankfully nothing too criminal has happened again. I tried to discuss this with Marilyn, but she won't even talk to me!"

Marilyn was the mayor's wife who had stopped attending the book club meetings. We think she is quite embarrassed by her husband's behavior.

Me: "The election date will be announced tomorrow. The paper received confirmation yesterday of that."

Norah: "Will Jed run? He has my vote!"

Me: "I don't know. He is a hard bird to read. I plan on visiting the pub later to get answers. Also, don't forget, the first meeting of the Cat Free Restful Roost is November 12. We will elect board members and plan our agenda."

Mary: "You see, Jed started that non profit for the good of the town! He would be a wonderful mayor! You tell him enough of the exploratory committee, the time is now to run!"

After a feisty discussion on whether Sarah Palin helped or set back the future of women in politics, I left the library for work. It was one of the slowest news days in a while, which I enjoyed, but Katherine paced the floors thinking of a new story idea. I left work and flew home early that day. Adam and I decided to have dinner at Jed's.

I needed an answer from Jed on his plans for mayor for the paper's lead story tomorrow on the election.

Jed: "What'll it be?"

Me: "Let me try an oyster sandwich."

Jed: "Wow, mixing it up a bit, huh? Adam, how about you?"

Adam: "Same for me!"

Jed: "Coming right up."

When Jed brought our sandwiches back he sat at the stool next to me.

Jed: "Susan, I have a very special announcement to make and I want you to write it up in the paper. Say I have a meeting at the community center at 7 p.m. tomorrow night. I heard the election date will be announced tomorrow as well so I might as well take the plunge."

Me: "I was hoping you would have news for me! I assume I know what the announcement will be, so I will keep my thoughts hush hush."

Jed: "Appreciate it! What do you think about ..."

Jed's question was interrupted by the police scanner. He had installed it so he could get a pulse on the town happenings. The recent bout of crimes in Restful Roost was one major reason for him thinking about running for mayor. The scanner called out a DIS code, which stood for disturbance. The location was a new church construction site.

Jed: "I will wrap this sandwich up for you."

Susan: "Thanks! Adam, don't wait up for me!"

I thanked Jed for the news scoop and I flew off to investigate.

I arrived at the location mentioned in the police call to find local architect Vincent Vulture arguing with a very loud Blue Jay. I saw Vincent's assistant Chad Cardinal standing nearby so I approached him to get the scoop.

Me: "Hey Chad, what is going on here? And who is that Blue Jay? I have never seen him before."

Chad: "That clown is a preacher from Pheasant Crest. His name is Jimmy Jay. He contracted us to build this huge megachurch, but hasn't paid us a single bill! Vincent has had enough and refuses to complete the building without back pay with interest. That didn't go over so well with Jimmy."

Me: "Wow! Do we even have enough birds here to fill a church this big?"

Chad: "I don't think it matters. He just wants the prestige!"

Me: "Oh look, here comes the mayor. He isn't flying quite right is he?"

Chad: "Yes, looks like he has been hitting the booze today."

After seeing the very unstable mayor arrive, Vincent Vulture and Jimmy Jay broke from their argument and walked over. Chad and I moved closer to listen in.

Vincent: "Mayor, thank you for arriving here so late. I know you must be quite busy having to deal with police matters as well as your mayoral duties. Chad and I were working late on this new project. In flew Jimmy Jay and he starts screeching at me to work faster, to hire more birds, and to use better materials. I have had enough of his verbal abuse! On top of that, he owes me ten thousand dollars! I refuse to continue working until I get my money!"

Jimmy started squawking and screaming.

Jimmy: "These are all lies. Birds go to hell when they lie. Look at the wood, it is all rotted!"

Vincent: "That is ridiculous. Mayor, go look at the building! I use quality products! Everybird knows that!"

Mayor Dove: "Whoa, whoa, whoa, everybird stop yelling. I have a splitting headache! Now, Vincent, this town needs religion. I mean, these crimes we have been having are a sign from above."

Jimmy: "Preach!"

Vincent: "What!? I can't continue working with this bird. He won't pay me!"

Jimmy: "You heard the mayor! Get back to work!"

Vincent: "You will not tell me what to do. I am off to talk to my lawyer!"

Vincent hissed loudly at both the mayor and Jimmy as he flew away. The mayor and Jimmy then huddled in a corner together talking quietly.

Me: "Chad, what is the deal with those two?"

Chad: "Not sure, but the mayor has been here every day ever since Jimmy got here. I think they are drinking buddies. I know one thing, I will never attend this church! Jimmy said I was vulgar because I have red feathers. I can't pick what color I am!"

Me: "Don't pay any attention to him. He seems a bit out of touch."

Chad: "Yes, and out of money!"

NEW CHURCH CONTROVERSY

ELECTION DAY SCHEDULED FOR NOVEMBER 20

JAEGER ANNOUNCEMENT TONIGHT

by Susan Towhee - Published November 5, 2022
in the Restful Roost Observer

Acting Police Chief (and mayor) Andrew Dove (current Chief Joe E. Finch is still missing) was alerted to a disturbance call at a new church construction site yesterday evening. Local architect Vincent Vulture and church owner Jimmy Jay had a heated disagreement on payment for the building.

Vincent Vulture had choice words for his client Jimmy. "Jimmy claims I am using rotted wood for the construction. I don't care if you want a church or a brothel, I will always use quality products and do my best work. He also says I should give him a discount because he is building a church. No way! I don't care who you are or what you do. You will pay the same as everybird else! If you ask me, he sounds like a regular charlatan. I should have never worked with him! We will settle this in court," said Vulture.

When asked for a comment Jimmy Jay also had choice words. "This town needs help and I am the one to give it. I will find another builder to complete this palace of worship. I refuse to pay for shoddy masonry. Also, Vincent Vulture's prices are outrageous. You should see the number he quoted me when I asked for gold plated walls and ceilings," said Jay.

The church was scheduled to be complete by Christmas, but that deadline is now up in the air.

Election day for mayor has been scheduled for November 20. Current Mayor Andrew Dove is up for re-election with no current contenders.

No mayoral candidates may change tonight as town resident and local business owner Jed Jaeger (owner of Jed's Pub) has a special announcement to make tonight at 7 p.m. at the Restful Roost Community Center. The deadline to file a run for mayor is tomorrow. All residents are automatically registered to vote and early voting will start one week prior to the election date.

Get out the vote Restful Roost!

Back at the Restful Roost Observer's office, Katherine and I were preparing for election coverage in the weeks to come when a very irate Jimmy Jay stormed in the building.

Jimmy: "I am going to sue this paper for libel!"

Katherine: "And what do you base that on?"

Jimmy: "That Vulture compared my church to a brothel!"

Katherine: "Well, you will have to take that up with him. He did show us past due invoices. We can print that tomorrow to clear things up if you like."

Jimmy: "No! How dare you! I am being targeted. Typical left wing media!"

And with that, he left.

Me: "Geez, that bird needs some meditation!"

Katherine: "Susan, check and see what you can find about this bird. I think an expose should be in order."

Later that night I attended Jed Jaeger's big announcement event at the community center. Anxious to see what he would say, I recorded the whole event. I had the feeling this was the beginning of a political odyssey that I knew the town needed! Here is Jed's speech transcript in full:

"Good evening, my fellow Restful Roosters! Thank you all for coming out here tonight. It shows you are all ready for a change in this town and you all are prepared to fight!

I can see we need to make some changes. Crime has risen and unqualified elected and appointed officials are either doing nothing about it or have no clue as to what to do. We also need more recreation options here which will draw in more tourists. We have a river and a lake we are not utilizing. We could install a boat dock or a waterpark. The ideas are endless!

I will end with this. I see a need for change. I am a local business owner. I am a concerned and caring citizen. Even though I have no past experience serving as an elected leader nor do I have a political science degree from a fancy eastern school like others, I do think I am capable of leading this town into the future.

I announce my candidacy for Mayor of Restful Roost and I ask all of you for your votes!"

At that point cheers erupted at the community center!

"HOORAH!"

"WIN WITH JED!"

"JED! JED!"

As the crowd mingled post speech, I spied Jimmy Jay lurking in the corner with the current mayor. Since the mayor was here I decided I better get a quote for the morning paper.

Me: "Hello Mayor Dove. I am surprised to see you here. Can I get a comment on the Jed for mayor announcement?"

Mayor Dove: "Well, you see, it's like this, umm, I just don't think birds like that should hold office."

Me: "Did you say 'birds like that?' Can you elaborate on what you mean by that?"

Jimmy: "Don't fall into the trap Mayor! These reporters will twist your words! Just tell her what we talked about, understand?"

Mayor Dove: "So sorry! Yes, you are right, Jimmy. Susan, I want to let you know that I have decided not to run for re-election and I will be throwing my support to Jimmy Jay for Mayor."

Me: "Excuse me? Jimmy is running for mayor? When was this announced? And he can't run for mayor. You have to be a citizen of this town."

Mayor Dove: "Well, I, uh, changed a few laws and now anybird can run for office no matter their residence."

At this moment Jed overheard our discussion and approached.

Jed: "What do you mean you changed the laws? Don't we have to vote on things like this?"

Mayor Dove: "This is why you are unqualified to run for mayor! There are certain things I can change on my own as mayor. It is a nice little benefit of the office."

Jed: "And that will be one of the first things I put an end to when I am elected."

Jimmy: "Not so fast you Parasitic Jaeger! I am going to be the next mayor."

Jed: "I am a Pomarine Jaeger, not a Parasitic Jaeger. And the town will be the judge of that."

Jimmy: "Oh, the town will have a lot to judge that is for sure. Oh and Sarah, is it? Please add in your paper that my church is open and ready for new congregants."

Jed: "Her name is Susan, and how can your church be ready if you don't even have the walls finished?"

Jimmy: "Don't you know that Jesus didn't need a building to teach the world?"

Jed: "Oh, brother, this bird thinks he is Jesus now. Didn't you want gold plated floors?"

Jimmy: "Kiss my cloaca!"

Before the conversation got any more heated, I decided to ask Jed to open his pub for a post speech celebration. I needed a bourbon neat before heading to the office to file my story.

JED JAEGER ANNOUNCES MAYORAL RUN

MAYOR WILL NOT RUN FOR RE-ELECTION

DOVE ENDORSES LOCAL PASTOR FOR MAYOR

DEBATE DATE SET FOR NOVEMBER 10

NEW CHURCH OPENS

by Susan Towhee - Published November 6, 2022
in the Restful Roost Observer

Yet another eventful evening last night in Restful Roost!

Local business owner Jed Jaeger announced to a packed crowd at the Restful Roost Community Center that he will be a candidate for mayor. His platform includes crime reduction and increasing tourism. "This town's government needs cleaning up and I am in to win," said Jaeger.

A bombshell in the election race last night was dropped when current Mayor Andrew Dove announced he will not seek re-election. He was vague on why he was dropping out but offered another surprise when he said he was throwing his support to another local businessbird, Jimmy Jay. According to an internal change in rules set by Mayor Dove, Jimmy is eligible to run despite not being a resident of Restful Roost. Jimmy's platform will be to lead the town to the Lord. "This town is not praying enough. There is too much crime and weird alien stuff going on here. If everybird will attend my new church I will show them the way," said Jay.

Now that candidates are set, Restful Roost Community Center Events Coordinator Charlene Chickadee has announced the first and only debate night set for 7 p.m. on November 10 at the community center. All residents are welcome and encouraged to attend. The moderator will be Katherine Heron, editor of the Restful Roost Observer.

As mentioned previously, Jimmy Jay's new church has opened. The location is a not yet completed building near the town square. Inaugural services will be held at 3 p.m. this afternoon.

Get out the vote Restful Roost!

Back in the office, Katherine and I discussed the events of last night.

Katherine: "Susan, how can that clown think he can win an election? Everybird thinks he is crazy and he doesn't even live here!"

Me: "I do think something fishy is going on. Why would the mayor bend the rules for an out of towner? Why are they so chummy?"

Katherine: "Did you know Jimmy is staying at the Presidential suite at the Restful Roost Inn?"

Me: "No way! That is like $1000 a night! You would think he could afford to pay Vincent Vulture!"

Katherine: "He is up to something for sure. We should go check out his church service today and see if we can find out further details."

Me: "Sounds like a plan!"

When we arrived at the church I saw it was very empty. Only Jimmy, Mayor Dove and two random birds were there. The building was nowhere near being complete. Scaffolding was still up, no working bathrooms were in sight, no handicap access anywhere, and no lights. Plenty of buckets were placed in the middle and at the end of every pew. Not to collect rain, though. These buckets were marked "Donations Only". Classy. Jimmy's sermon, or lecture more like it, lasted only a few minutes. It was filled with lots of talk on hell, sin, and the end times. The finale was a call to fill the donation buckets before we left. Double classy.

After the speech, Jimmy and Mayor Dove went to the back office together and we approached the other birds to see who they were and to get a quote or two for the paper. I approached and noticed they were wearing comically large hats and coats.

Me: "Excuse me ladies, would either of you care to comment with thoughts on the church or the services today?"

They both turned and were about to walk away.

Me: "Excuse me? Can I get a quote please?"

One of the birds turned around and took off her hat.

Goldy: "Oh hell, Susan, it's me and Norah!"

Me: "What are you two doing here?"

Norah: "We just had to see what the fuss was about. A cousin of mine told me to watch out for this Jimmy bird. Said he nearly bankrupted the town!"

Katherine: "What do you mean bankrupted the town? Was this Pheasant Crest?"

Norah: "No it was Thistle Thicket. She said he made deals with the town mayor there to get tax breaks on his churches and other investments. The mayor was using town funds and got caught. They are still trying to get out of the red."

Me: "Oh boy, now I see why he is so chummy with Mayor Dove."

Goldy: "Can we discuss all the gold jewelry he was wearing at the podium? I was getting a headache from the glare! And those dyed feathers? Dude, you are a BLUE JAY. Why dye all of your feathers white?"

Katherine: "Maybe he is channeling his inner televangelist?"

Norah: "Get this, Jimmy Jay isn't even his real name. He also has multiple ex-wives, homes in other cities besides Thistle Thicket and Pheasant Crest, and several failed gourmet bird food lines."

Katherine: "Geez, what a loser. Susan, I say this needs priority investigation! Go fly to those towns and see what you can find."

Through November 7-9 I took a trip to both Thistle Thicket and Pheasant Crest to investigate. I took my mate Adam with me so we could have a vacation/research trip. We stayed at a secluded cabin equal distance between both towns. During the day I visited with the local police, newspaper, coffee house, etc. to gain intel. At night we had pizza and wine, smoked cigars outside with a glass of bourbon, played board games, or watched movies.

I learned that Jimmy Jay, aka Matt Jay, aka Rudy Jay was committed once for insanity, was investigated for money laundering, arrested for illegal picketing, and investigated for bribery.

Once I verified some sources, this would be a hot story!

The day was November 10, debate day. Before the debate I decided to visit Jimmy Jay at his room in the Restful Roost Inn to get a comment on my findings.

Jimmy: "I have no comment. Those are, once again, all lies by the left wing media! I will win this election because I am the savior this town needs! Here is a button for you!"

He then threw his campaign button at me and slammed the door in my face. I think I hit a nerve.

Back at the office Katherine was pleased with my investigation.

Katherine: "Great work! Jimmy sounds like a real class act."

Me: "I don't know why so many birds fall for this crap."

Katherine: "Swindlers are everywhere! Finalize your report. Tomorrow we will lead with the debate and then the next day we will print the expose. Who knows, maybe more will be uncovered tomorrow!"

Katherine was a regular newshound. She could smell a juicy story!

Chaos would be the only word to describe what happened at the debate. A transcript and description of the melee would be the only true way to explain what was said and done. Here goes:

Moderator Katherine Heron: "Good evening Restful Roosters and welcome to the first and only mayoral debate. My name is Katherine Heron and I am the editor of the local newspaper, the Restful Roost Observer. I will be your moderator this evening. The two candidates are local business owners Jed Jaeger and Jimmy Jay."

Jed: "Local, my ass!"

Katherine: "Please, no interruptions! The two candidates will get equal time for questions and time for closing comments. The debate will last one hour. Mr. Jay, the first question will go to you. Mr. Jay, why do you think you are qualified to run for mayor of a town you do not reside in?"

Jimmy: "Look, Jennifer, I am a bird of the cloth. It matters not where I reside. My teachings will bring this town into the light. I could run for mayor of Miami if I wanted to, but I have chosen this special town of Resting Roost."

Katherine: "The name of the town is actually Restful Roost and my name, once again, is Katherine. Mr. Jaeger, why do you want to be mayor?"

Jed: "Please call me Jed, Katherine. This town has a

crime problem. I want to be the bird that changes that. I will do a nationwide search to hire a well qualified police chief. This town also needs to show off its best assets. We have great water facilities that we need to put to use. We have a world class hotel and community center. By promoting those things we can bring in more tourists to generate revenue. I want to lead the town I live in and love into a better and brighter future. I want to be the mayor because I care."

Katherine: "The next question goes to Mr. Jay. What are your opinions on..."

Before Katherine could finish her question a commotion occurred at the back of the room. A very blond American Goldfinch approached Jimmy Jay and started screaming:

"Rudy! There you are! You lying, cheating, no good fowl! Why are you up on stage? Where is my alimony money?"

Jimmy: "Please Becky, not here. I am in the middle of something. Can't we discuss this later?"

Becky: "I don't know what you are up to now, but I want my money!"

A yell from Vincent Vulture in the crowd: "Get in line, lady!"

Becky: "Oh I see, you owe birds in this town money now? That's it! I'm getting a lawyer!"

As quick as she was there, she was gone.

Katherine: "Care to explain that Mr. Jay?"

Jimmy: "Uh, I think the next question is for Jed, not me."

Katherine: "Was that lady your ex-wife? Why did she call you Rudy?"

Jimmy: "I don't know who that bird was, but I will pray for her."

Katherine: "Ok, moving on. Jed, what are your opinions on invasive species and how can we best control them?"

Jed: "Thanks for the question. As everybird here knows, we had a crime earlier this year involving cowbirds. I recommend, once our new police chief is hired, that we have nightly patrols. The night patrols will make sure our nests are safe and that no suspicious activity occurs."

Katherine: "Mr. Jay, same question."

Jimmy: "Well I think the invasive species problem is standing right next to me."

"Boos!" and "That's uncalled for!" rained from the crowd.

Katherine: "Please, no interruptions. That goes for the crowd as well! Continue Mr. Jay."

Jimmy: "I was told there were migrating bird murders here recently and confusion exists on who did it. I think it was this jaeger standing next to me. He was hungry for bird meat and he killed them!"

More "boos" and "Shut up!" chants exploded from the crowd.

Jimmy: "I know you all are thinking it! You say it was a cat, but how can you all be so sure. How can you all sleep at night knowing a predator who is hungry for birds lives among us?"

Cries from the crowd of "He's crazy" and "It was a cat!" came from the crowd.

Katherine: "Please, we need to have order here! Jed, how do you reply to these allegations?"

There was silence as we waited for Jed to calm down and compose his thoughts.

Jed: "I have a secret and I want the town to know it tonight."

Jimmy: "See, I told you! He is a murderer!"

Katherine: "Silence! Continue Jed."

Jed: "The day I was released from jail for being incorrectly accused of murdering innocent birds, I went to find the cat. I found it. Then, I murdered it and dragged the body to the town square."

Gasps from all in the crowd erupted!

Katherine: "You are saying that you killed a cat with no help?"

Jed: "Well, I am a predator, I will admit that. The cat was no problem for me. If it made the town safer, I had to do it. Up north I would eat small rodents from time to time, but never birds. The meat is nasty. Besides, I would never judge another bird based on their background. As mayor, I would welcome all immigrants!

The crowd became out of control. Chants of "JED!" erupted. There was no way this was an even contest now. Katherine had no choice but to end the debate.

CANDIDATE JAEGER ADMITS TO CAT MURDER

JAEGER CLEAR WINNER IN DEBATE

DEBATE DISRUPTION FROM EX-WIFE OF JAY

by Susan Towhee - Published November 11, 2022 in the Restful Roost Observer

A shocking admission was revealed last night at the mayoral debate. Jed Jaeger, candidate for mayor, admitted he terminated the life of the cat responsible for local migrating bird murders. His reasoning was to make the town safer.

Exit polling has Jed with an astounding 95% approval rating and the clear winner of the debate.

The revelation occurred after Jimmy Jay accused Jed of murdering the birds.

Jay had to face an outburst from the crowd from an ex-wife who was demanding back alimony pay. The Restful Roost Observer has recently obtained more details into the personal and professional life of Jimmy Jay. The full story will appear in tomorrow's edition.

Get out the vote Restful Roost!

I decided to have lunch at Jed's so I could gauge reaction to the debate. Jed was beaming and pouring beers when I arrived.

Me: "Hey, Jed, did you see the results of the exit poll? 95% approval!"

Jed: "95%? Who were the other 5%? What is their problem with me?"

Me: "Well, volunteers did say the younger voters polled had comments like 'not cool enough' and 'he doesn't think like me' so I wouldn't worry about it. 95% is unprecedented!"

Jed: "Screw that, I want 100% approval. Damn millennials. I need to think of something."

With that, he walked off to contemplate.

Back at the office I was finalizing my report on Jimmy Jay when Jed walked in.

Me: "What can we help you with here at the paper?"

Jed: "I thought of a way to get the millennial vote. Parlor Pigeon Wrestling!"

Katherine: "Uh, that is stupid."

Jed: "No, it is cool and they will love it. Please add it in the paper tomorrow as one of my campaign pledges."

Me: "Jed, those birds have issues and making them fight is a bit barbaric."

Jed: "No, it is cool and that is what the public wants."

Katherine: "Well, we can add it, but in fairness, we need to ask Jimmy if he has anything to announce."

Katherine asked me to fly over to his suite at the Inn to check. I didn't think it would do much good. Maybe I could get a button for Katherine...

At the Inn, I ran into the owner, Peter Woodpecker.

Peter: "Hey, Susan, are you here to see that Blue Jay?"

Me: "Yep! Why do you ask?"

Peter: "If he answers the door for you, tell him he has twenty-four hours to leave or I will forcibly remove him. He won't answer my calls or pecks and he owes me for two nights!"

Me: "Yikes, I will let him know. He doesn't have a great track record on payments I have noticed."

Turns out I was able to get a comment from Jimmy as I claimed I had complimentary champagne from the mayor and he opened the door.

Jimmy: "Oh, it's you. What do you want?"

Me: "I wanted to know if you had any special announcements to print in the paper. Jed has a new campaign pledge and we are offering you the same opportunity."

Jimmy: "Oh, um, yes, I pledge to deport all non native birds and ban liquor."

Me: "Ban liquor? You just opened the door for free champagne."

Jimmy: "Well, it will be banned when I become mayor."

Me: "Ok, any comment on your ex-wife's allegations or other town investigations? We have a major story to hit tomorrow and would love a comment."

Jimmy: "NO COMMENT! I bet that jaeger was behind that bird disrupting the debate as well. Now, go away!"

Me: "Oh, the hotel says you will be kicked out in twenty-four hours if you don't pay."

The door was slammed in my face. No free button today.

JAEGER PROMISES PARLOR PIGEON WRESTLING

JAY WILL BAN LIQUOR

CFRR INAUGURAL MEETING TONIGHT

by Susan Towhee - Published November 12, 2022
in the Restful Roost Observer

New campaign promises were announced yesterday from the two candidates for mayor of Restful Roost.

Jed Jaeger will bring Parlor Pigeon wrestling to town. "I hope this exciting recreational sport will draw in the younger crowds," said Jaeger.

Jimmy Jay told the Observer that he will deport all non-native birds as well as ban liquor.

The observer will monitor the town's reaction to these campaign promises and will report any new pledges.

Citizens are encouraged to attend the first meeting of the Cat Free Restful Roost (CFRR) non profit at 5 p.m. tonight at the Restful Roost Community Center.

Get out the vote Restful Roost!

The first meeting of the Cat Free Restful Roost (CFRR) at the community center was quite productive. A large number of town residents were in attendance. The first order of business was to name board members and create a plan of action. Jed was named Board Chair, Thea was named Board Secretary, Norah was named Board Treasurer, and I was named Board Vice-Chair.

Jed: "Norah, how can we start fundraising? Can't do anything until we have cash."

Norah: "We can ask for grants, do a mail campaign, set up booths at local businesses, a variety of things. Then, we can proceed with national outreach."

Jed: "Great, get to work on that! Susan, what should our priorities be? First off, the new police chief will be trained on cats so they know what to look for. That is, if I am elected mayor."

Susan: "I have no doubt you will be elected! I like that idea as well as working with the Cornell Lab of Ornithology on local education about cats. Education is key. Once birds know what to look for then we can start on actions."

Thea: "I have all of these ideas typed up and I will send

them to you all digitally. We should think about how to communicate proper cat ownership to humans as well."

Jed: "Another great idea!"

After a bit more discussion, I headed back to the office to work on my story. I found Katherine still at work as usual. Soon after I arrived we had a visitor with a shocking admission.

Mayor Dove showed up at the Observer office surprisingly a bit sober.

Katherine: "How can we help you tonight?"

Mayor Dove: "I need to speak with the paper to clear things up. The nasty politics has gone too far. I also want to confirm that I took bribes from Jimmy Jay so he could get his new church property for a bargain and a tax free exemption status. When I started to have doubts, he then started to blackmail me. Said he was going to spread it around town that I was having an affair. If that wasn't enough, I was recently visited by special agents from the Bird Tax Service and they are also investigating him. I just want a clean slate before I retire."

Katherine: "Mayor, I promise you a fair write up because of your honesty. Sad to see you leave, but it is time. Can you stay and provide more details to Susan?"

Mayor Dove: "Yes. I thank you both for your dedication to journalism. I will be leaving the day after the election to Florida for retirement. Marilyn deserves a fresh start as well."

After a lengthy interview I said my goodbyes to the

mayor. When the mayor left, Katherine turned to me and let out a huge celebratory whoop.

Katherine: "What a story! God, this must be what Ben Bradlee felt back in 1974! Confirm his story, especially the Bird Tax Service bit and print it, Susan!"

Later that night my mate Adam surprised me with dinner out at the new restaurant at the Inn.

Me: "What did I do to deserve this outing?"

Adam: "You have been working so hard lately. I thought you deserved a treat."

Me: "How sweet!"

Adam: "I also have one more surprise for you."

Adam presented her with an envelope. I was shocked when I opened it!

Me: "Front row balcony tickets to see the Valentino Vogelkop Superb Bird-of-Paradise show! This must have cost a fortune!"

Adam: "Business has been good lately, so why not! You only live once!"

We finished a bottle of Highland Manor Merlot and headed home.

EXCLUSIVE REPORTING ON JIMMY JAY:

INVOLVED IN LOCAL BLACKMAIL SCHEME

IRS INVESTIGATION CONFIRMED

by Susan Towhee - Published November 13, 2022
in the Restful Roost Observer

The Restful Roost Observer has an exclusive story on candidate for mayor Jimmy Jay.

After extensive reporting it has been found that Jay:

- owes alimony to at least three ex-wives
- has main residences listed in Thistle Thicket, Pheasant Crest, Restful Roost, New Jersey, and Palm Beach
- has been sued eight times for food poisoning from his failed "Jay's Best" gourmet bird seed line
- has tax records listed under the names Matt Jay and Rudy Jay
- was committed once for insanity at the Portland, OR Home for Quirky Birds
- arrested five times for illegal picketing in various towns

Jay is also currently under local investigation for bribery and blackmail of an elected official. According to Restful Roost Mayor Andrew Dove, Jimmy Jay approached him to offer campaign funds in exchange for a tax deal on his new church. "Jimmy told me it wasn't right that Restful Roost makes churches pay taxes. He offered me money for my re-election campaign in exchange for a tax free property. When I refused he said he would tell the town that I paid for an underage Ruby Throated Hummingbird to provide me with company. He also told me to drop out of the mayor's race and then endorse him! I felt I had no choice," said Dove.

The Observer has also verified that the BTS (Bird Tax Service) is investigating Jay for tax evasion. Since the investigation is ongoing no further details can be provided.

The Observer reached out to Jimmy Jay for comment on the recent developments, but he provided no comment.

The shockwaves of the story hit the town all day. No comment was received from Jimmy Jay, who had apparently cleared out all of his possessions at the church. Restful Roost Inn owner Peter Woodpecker said he left without paying. Peter also says he will pursue legal action.

Katherine and I decide to have lunch at Jed's to congratulate ourselves on the story.

Jed: "Ladies, great story today!"

Katherine: "Thanks! Mealworm sandwiches and two beers please!"

Jed: "Coming right up!"

At that moment a group of high school kids marched in the bar with signs that read:

"Stop Pigeon Abuse!"

"Say No to Pigeon Wrestling!"

"Anti-brutality!"

Jed: "What is this mess! Hey, no underage birds are allowed in here!"

Youth 1: "We are not here to drink. We are here as voting age citizens expressing our disgust with Parlor Pigeon wrestling!"

Jed: "Have you seen the videos? It is the new 'in' thing!"

Youth 2: "No, it isn't! It is bird abuse!"

Jed: "Abuse? Says who?"

Youth 3: "Says the ACLU!"

Jed: "You birds really aren't that excited about it?"

Youth 1: "No! Take back your pledge!"

Jed: "I only brought it up because I thought the millennials would think it was cool."

Youth 2: "Dude, that is thoughtful, but just ask us what we want."

Jed: "Ok, what do you want?"

Youth 2:"How about we have a meeting to discuss it?"

Jed: "Alright, how about tonight at Norah's Café at 7 p.m.? I can call and ask her to stay open late so we have the place to ourselves."

Youth 3: "We will be there! So you will announce the pigeon thing is off?"

Jed: "Ugh, yes. If that is your desire."

The now happy youth group walked out. I hoped Jed would not create another crazy scheme for votes. His best strategy was to stay silent until the election was over!

JAEGER WALKS BACK PIGEON WRESTLING

NEW JAEGER CAMPAIGN PLEDGES

JAY SKIPS TOWN

SUPERB BIRD-OF-PARADISE SHOW SOLD OUT

by Susan Towhee - Published November 14, 2022
in the Restful Roost Observer

Mayoral candidate Jed Jaeger has renounced his campaign pledge to bring Parlor Pigeon wrestling to Restful Roost. After a meeting with local youth last night Jaeger said "I can now see that the pigeon wrestling idea was wrong. The birds are mistreated and events that showcase their disabilities would send a wrong message."

After a two hour discussion with a local youth group, Jed has added the following campaign pledges to his platform: free health care for all, pro immigration, and a monthly town cleanup day.

Mayoral candidate Jimmy Jay has fled the town amidst BTS investigation reporting. His last known whereabouts was the Restful Roost Inn. Owner Peter Woodpecker said "He left without paying me and his room is trashed. I am offering a free weekend stay if anybird knows his current location." If anybird has information on Jimmy Jay please call the BTS at 1-800-TAX-BIRD.

The Restful Roost Community Center would like the town to know that the Fabulous Dancing Valentino Vogelkop Superb Bird-of-Paradise show tomorrow night is now sold out. For those birds who have not seen this extraordinary talent, check out his YouTube page where you will find magnificent dances and breathtaking displays.

Get out the vote Restful Roost!

In the days leading up to election day, Jed held a couple more rallies. His win was sure to be in the bag now with the only other opponent nowhere to be seen.

On the night of the election pretty much the whole town was at a watch party at the community center. Flags and bunting hung from every rafter. Signs were everywhere with Jed's campaign slogan "In to Win!" written on them. The crowd was entertained by a special acoustic performance from Edgar Raven of The Ravens. At about 9 p.m. the results were in. Jed won with 100% of the vote!

After the results were announced and Jed gave his victory speech, Mayor Dove approached the podium and offered his congratulations to Jed and thanked the town for their previous support. He then apologized to the town for his recent crimes and requested that he step down immediately and have Jed be sworn in on the spot. With a unanimous vote of yes from the crowd, Jed was sworn in as the next mayor of Restful Roost.

The crowd exited the community center and to the town square where fireworks lit up the sky. My mate Adam brought over the finest cigars from our collection and we gave one to Mayor Jaeger in celebration!

JED JAEGER WINS MAYOR RACE

SWORN IN IMMEDIATELY

by Susan Towhee - Published November 21, 2022
in the Restful Roost Observer

Restful Roost has a new mayor. Last night the town (literally the entire town) voted for Jed Jaeger for Mayor.

Ex-mayor Andrew Dove thanked the town for the opportunity to serve and asked that Jed be sworn in immediately.

Mayor Jaeger has plans to get started right away. "Big thanks to Edgar Raven for the entertainment tonight. And super big thanks to the town of Restful Roost! I love my new home and I can't wait for the future. Let's all party the night away tonight, but tomorrow, the work starts," said Jaeger.

Excitement was in the air as new leadership took over in Restful Roost. Andrew Dove worked out a deal with the BTS to avoid jail time. He and Marilyn Dove left town for their retirement home in Florida. A few days after the election Jimmy Jay was found at the US/Canadian border and was arrested. It is doubtful that anybird will get their money back from him at this point. Once the arrest was announced Mayor Jaeger approved the demolition of the church and allowed Vincent Vulture to keep the land and do with it what he likes. The mayor also announced the search for a new police chief. Mayor Jaeger's final act as mayor in his first week was to send the remainder of the money from his campaign war chest to the Rescue Parlor Pigeons charity.

Just another day in Restful Roost!

~ 6 ~

IT'S A WONDERFUL NEST

The Story (as I remember it)...

It was Xmas Eve around midnight and all was quiet. Except for the police scanner blaring a BURG (burglary) call at the community center! My mate, Adam, and I had just arrived home from a special holiday themed spoken word play and musical at the center. Local actor Hopper Cottontail and country music star Grant Goose performed a play that depicted Cottontail's alien experience and how the teachings of love from the aliens is something to keep in mind this holiday season. The center's event coordinator, Charlene Chickadee, promoted an Xmas bird seed drive for the needy before the show. When I left the boxes were overflowing. Hopefully the burglary was not related to that! So much for a long winter's nap! Off I flew in a flash!

When I arrived at the community center I saw my cousin, Vanessa Sparrow. What was she doing here, I had wondered.

Here is a little background on Vanessa:

She grew up in town with me and my other sparrow cousins. While I am an Eastern Towhee, she is a House Sparrow. We are related to other sparrows in town, too. From what I know she has had at least five boyfriends and at least three kids with each. She has had about twenty different nest sites including behind a human home's broken shutter, an old boot by the river, and one behind a streetlight. Her hobby is stealing things from human garages when the door is open. Not sure if she sells the items or keeps the stuff for herself. Her idol is Tanya Tucker. You all remember Tucker's classic song "Two Sparrows in a Hurricane" from the 90's? Well, Vanessa has a tattoo of Tanya next to a hurricane on her wing.

I have offered her a place to stay many times so she can get her life together along with a job cleaning Adam and I's rental properties, but she refuses my help. The money I used to send her every spring however, was never refused. I knew she would need cash when a new brood was hatched before summer. A year ago, I stopped sending it because I was tired of never getting a thank you.

As I approached I saw Vanessa had birdcuffs on and was being interrogated by our new police chief, Millard Mallard. Millard was appointed by Mayor Jaeger after a very intense nationwide search. Millard was police chief in Marquette, MI for about fifteen years. He wanted warmer climates and a change of scenery, plus his experience investigating a bird trafficking ring around the Great Lakes also helped boost his credentials.

Me: "Hey chief! Can you tell me what my cousin has done now?"

Chief Mallard: "Hey there! Yep, those hidden cameras I have installed all over town helped me catch this one. Looks like she broke into the center and was attempting to steal the bird seed cache that birds donated. Caught her in the act! Problem is, she won't talk."

Me: "Oh boy. Vanessa! Stealing at Christmas? This is a new low!"

Vanessa eyed me and then started to scream such vulgarities that cannot be repeated in this story.

Chief Mallard: "All right, calm down, calm down. I will haul her off to the station so she can think about her actions. Already called Charlene to give her an update and told her I would lock up. It's late and it's Christmas Eve. When she is ready to talk I will reach out to the paper."

And with that, Chief Mallard and Vanessa flew off to jail. Thieving at Christmas! What a shame. At least the seed was saved. Tomorrow I hoped to get to the bottom of this.

ATTEMPTED THEFT AT COMMUNITY CENTER

DONATED SEED SAFE

by Susan Towhee - Published December 25, 2022
in the Restful Roost Observer

Last night a break in was reported at the Restful Roost Community Center after hours. The thief was identified as Vanessa Sparrow. Her plan was to steal bird seed that was donated by attendees at the Restful Roost Christmas show. Thanks to the newly installed hidden cameras Police Chief Millard Mallard was alerted and made it to the scene as Vanessa was loading up. Vanessa has been arrested and is awaiting judgment at the local jail. Chief Mallard stated that he will determine punishment after the holidays.

Watch what you do Restful Roost! Cameras are watching!

Disclosure: Vanessa Sparrow is a cousin of Restful Roost Observer reporter Susan Towhee.

Despite the festive holiday, I couldn't get Vanessa out of my mind. No one should be away from family for the holidays. Well, I guess if you break the law you should.

Vanessa was family, though. After lunch and gift exchange with my mate, I decided to fly to the jail with leftovers to see what details we could get. Maybe a night in the slammer helped Vanessa see the light.

We arrived to find Vanessa with the chief eating pie, listening to a Frank Sinatra Christmas playlist, and having what seemed like a good time.

Me: "Hey chief, what is going on here?"

Chief Mallard: "Susan, I have learned that if you show a little kindness birds will open up and start to talk."

I gave the chief a side glance.

Chief Mallard: "I took police community outreach training up in Michigan. Vanessa, why don't you tell your cousin here your story."

Vanessa: "Oh Susan, I just can't catch a break. I lost my job, my boyfriend flew off, and I have a nest full of young-ins that need food. I was desperate!"

Always excuses from her. I gave her a confused look.

Me: "Vanessa, shouldn't your kids already be gone? This is December. They are grownups now! And why didn't you call me instead of stealing? We were collecting food for the needy, which is birds just like you!"

Vanessa: "Here we go again!"

Chief Mallard: "Now Vanessa, let's be calm and share our feelings. Susan was only trying to ask why you didn't reach out for help instead of breaking the law. Remember what we talked about."

Vanessa: "All right, I get it. Look, I am embarrassed, ok.

I am tired of being looked at as trashy. I know birds judge House Sparrows. We can't all be a fancy towhee like you."

Me: "Vanessa, I would hardly call myself fancy. I have brown feathers just like you."

Vanessa: "Oh no, you have pretty rufous sides and milk chocolate brown head feathers. You're fancy."

Me: "Well, who cares what birds look like! It is their behavior that matters! Maybe we can help you find a job. Does that sound good?"

Vanessa: "I ain't qualified to do anything."

Chief Mallard: "I spoke with the community center coordinator, Charlene, and she was talking about how busy she was and needed help. Let's see if you can work with her?"

Vanessa: "Yea, right, like she will give me a job after I stole seed from there."

Chief Mallard: "Just let me deal with it. If you are true about wanting to change then it will all work out."

Either the chief is a miracle worker or a Christmas miracle was about to happen and Vanessa had truly changed. Time will tell.

Incredibly, the chief decided to release Vanessa from the jail yesterday, so I paid for a room at the Restful Roost Inn for her to spend the night. The chief put a leg band tracking device on her in case she tried to fly off. She still had to face charges. Since we had snow on the ground it was difficult to locate food, so, Adam and I decided to get breakfast at Norah's Café. From the looks of the crowd, we weren't the only birds with that idea. We spotted a table near Goldy, Mary, Charlene, and Thea.

Me: "Good morning ladies! Quite the snowfall out there, huh?"

Thea: "Yes, it is pretty bad. I decided to close the library today. Not many birds out the day after Xmas, anyway."

Goldy: "Any news on what will happen to Vanessa, Susan?"

Me: "Well, she was released from jail, but she has a tracker on. Chief said he was going to you, Charlene, if you could get her a job."

Charlene: "I was so angry at her, but the chief has a calming way about him. I do need help at the center. What skills do you think she has?"

Me: "Skills? Oh my, um..."

I could think of not one thing.

Adam: "Well, she definitely knows how to collect and sort things. Maybe she can be a stockroom assistant?"

Charlene: "Good thinking, Adam."

Me: "The other issue is where she will stay. If she builds a nest on her own then it will be condemned by the town. She needs a nice place to live while she gets her life back on track."

Mary: "I heard that Vincent Vulture was planning on starting a non profit charity with the land he was granted by the town after that Blue Jay fiasco. Rumor is he wants to start a Nests for Humanity type organization since he has contracting experience."

Goldy: "What a cool idea! Maybe his first test subject should be Vanessa. The town can pitch in!"

Me: "This might work, ladies and gent! Adam, after breakfast let's visit Vincent's office to get the scoop."

After a yummy suet cake at Norah's, Adam and I stopped at Vincent's Visions to discuss his new business. Vincent agreed that Vanessa would be a good candidate, as long as she put in her fair share of the work. The non profit would be called Nest for Avians. He said him and his assistant Chad Cardinal would go talk with her and get details squared away. If all went well I could announce it in the paper tomorrow. It would be the town's first nest raising!

VULTURE LAUNCHES NON PROFIT

HELP NEEDED FOR INAUGURAL NEST BUILD

by Susan Towhee - Published December 27, 2022
in the Restful Roost Observer

Restful Roost has a new non profit in town. Vincent Vulture, owner of Vincent's Visions, has announced the launch of Nest for Avians. The organization will supply building materials and help with construction of nests for needy birds. Birds participating in the program will be asked to work 5 hours a day on the project to gain a sense of ownership and pride in the new home. "I am glad to give back to the community in this way. My architecture skills will come in handy as I help those less fortunate build a solid, reliable, and beautiful new nest," said Vulture.

To kick off this endeavor the town is urged to participate in the first nest build. Vanessa Sparrow has agreed to work on building her new home in Restful Roost and she hopes the community will forgive her for the recent attempted theft and help with the nest build. "I know I got a lot to prove, but if the town will give me a chance, I promise I will change," said Sparrow.

A meeting to go over details is set for tonight at 5 p.m. at the Restful Roost Community Center.

Later that evening at the center, it was standing room only as the town showed up in force!

Mayor Jed Jaeger provided opening remarks and gave thanks to Vincent for his non profit. It was decided that the nest could be built within two days if the weather cooperated. Since we are in the South, the snow we had earlier melted. It was now an unseasonably 70 degrees out!

Vanessa gave a surprisingly sincere apology to the crowd. She even hugged Vincent and cried a bit.

Before the meeting concluded Charlene announced she had a few comments.

Charlene: "Thank you all for showing up tonight. As everybird knows I have been a bit slammed here at the community center. That is why I offered a job as assistant to Vanessa Sparrow. She would assist with various projects around the building and help with marketing. Oh, and she has accepted!"

A hearty round of clapping went up from the crowd.

Charlene: "That's not all of the news I have! I was on the phone today finalizing details on an upcoming show with the artist and I brought up that I would be busy the next couple of days. When she asked why I told her the details. She has agreed to donate money to the non profit and she will offer a free ticket to her show for all who participate in the nest build. I am talking about non other than *rachel*."

Gasps and cheers erupted from the crowd!

Charlene: "For those who live in an abandoned bower nest, *rachel* is a Superb Fairywren singing phenomenon who will be performing at our New Year's Eve show here at the center. Your ticket will be presented at the nest opening. Remember, you have to put in at least ten hours to qualify. Thanks Restful Roost!"

TOWN RALLIES TO HELP WITH NEST BUILD

COMMUNITY CENTER NEW HIRE

SINGING VIRTUOSO *rachel* ASSISTS

MAYORS' FIRST TOWN MEETING TONIGHT

by Susan Towhee - Published December 28, 2022
in the Restful Roost Observer

Restful Roost residents are anxious to get started with the Nest for Avians nest build. The nest construction will start on December 29 with a two day goal of completion. "With this many birds helping, we can definitely be ready by the 29th. I am honored and pleased that this many birds are on board for this," said Nest for Avians founder Vincent Vulture.

Two surprises were publicized last night when Restful Roost Community Center Events Coordinator Charlene Chickadee announced that Vanessa Sparrow will start work at the center as an assistant. The other surprise of the night was that singing phenom *rachel* will be donating a ticket to all birds who participate in the nest raising. "*rachel* was very excited to help out. She always supports worthy causes and we are thankful for her support," said Chickadee.

rachel will be performing this New Year's Eve at the community center. Tickets are now sold out due to *rachel*'s gift, so be sure to sign up to work at Nest for Avians to get a ticket. It will be THE event for New Year's!

Mayor Jed Jaeger has announced his first town

meeting to be held tonight at 7 p.m. at the community center. "Details on funding for my new programs will be announced. I hope everybird can attend," said Jaeger.

The town buzzed as it prepared for the build that would start tomorrow. Most businesses had planned to close for the day so their staff could assist with the nest. First stop for me was the town library for our weekly book club meeting. That week's book was *Death of a Christmas Caterer* by Lee Hollis. After an enthusiastic discussion on which Hollis book was the best (no way to pick, in my opinion), I stopped by the office to do more work. For lunch, I picked up a bag lunch at Jed's Pub, went back to the office, and then it was time for Jed's first meeting as Mayor!

It was another packed night at the community center! I spotted Vanessa setting up extra chairs and headed her way.

Me: "Hi Vanessa, how are things?"

Vanessa: "Oh, this is so much fun, Susan! I am getting exercise walking around. I do litter cleanups outside. I even help answer the phone! Guess who I talked to today!?"

Me: "An upcoming performer I would guess?"

Vanessa: "Oh yes, I talked to Johnny Warbler from the

Tennessee Warblers! They want to plan for a show next year!"

Me: "Get out! He is so cool!"

Vanessa: "I know! Everything is working out here. A couple of my kids said they will come and visit the new nest. I told them no free-loading, though! It is time for them to get a job of their own."

Me: "Good for you! And you know you are welcome anytime at my nest."

Vanessa: "Yes, I will see you more often, I promise. Will you be at the nest build?"

Me: "Of course! I am scheduled for all day tomorrow!"

Vanessa: "Awesome! I will see you then. Back to work for me!"

Vanessa walked off to get more chairs and get the microphones working on the stage. It was so good to see her happy! Soon after 7:15 Mayor Jaeger took the stage. Here we go!

Mayor Jaeger: "Welcome Restful Roost! I will keep this brief because I value your time. Here are a few dates for you. On January 1 all residents will be automatically enrolled in free health care. On January 5 we will have our first town cleanup date. Meet at the town square at dawn. How will we pay for this you all are wondering? On January 2 windmills will be installed. They will generate enough power to not only supply our needs, but we can sell it to neighboring towns for a profit. Open to any questions."

A thunderous applause burst from the crowd.

"Yea, that is what we elected you for!"

"Hurrah for Mayor Jed!"

The Mayor answered every single question thrown at him. He was definitely prepared for this job. After an hour or so, he called an end to the meeting and wished Vanessa and the town luck on the nest build.

MAYOR DELIVERS ON HEALTH CARE

FIRST TOWN CLEANUP DATE ANNOUNCED

NEST BUILD STARTS TODAY

by Susan Towhee - Published December 29, 2022
in the Restful Roost Observer

Restful Roost residents were pleasantly shocked at the first mayoral town meeting last night when Mayor Jed Jaeger announced free healthcare to start on January 1. The costs will be virtually nothing after the profits roll in from new windmills that will be installed on January 2. The towns of Thistle Thicket and Pheasant Crest will buy energy from us which will offset the cost of the healthcare costs. "No one saw this coming. We thought maybe taxes would be raised. Couldn't be happier," said resident Chad Cardinal. Residents can stop by the health clinic for details.

Also announced last night was the date of the first town cleanup. Residents should meet at dawn at the town square on January 5. This is a rain or shine event. Bags and gloves will be supplied.

Reminder that today is the first day of the Nests for Avians nest build. Meet at the old church lot to begin work.

Get fired up Restful Roost!

The day of the nest build started strong. The turnout was great and the weather was perfect. Norah's Café and Jed's Pub donated food and drink to the workers. By the afternoon it was announced by Vincent that we were already over halfway done. He sent us home so we could get a good night's sleep for the final day of building tomorrow. Never had I been so tired! After a quick homemade squid sandwich for dinner, I sipped some bourbon and I was off to sleep! The next day was just as busy, but by 5 p.m. the nest was complete! Chad set up a giant robin egg blue ribbon around the nest. Mayor Jaeger, Vincent, and Vanessa all held the giant scissors to pose for pictures and to snap the ribbon. The crowd was jubilant yet very tired! Vincent told the crowd he would hoist the nest up and install it in a tree near the community center.

NEST FOR AVIANS NEST COMPLETE

NEW OWNER SPARROW GRATEFUL

CHARGES DROPPED AGAINST SPARROW

rachel SHOW TONIGHT

by Susan Towhee - Published December 31, 2022
in the Restful Roost Observer

Thanks to Restful Roost residents, a bird has a new home! Completion ended at around 5 p.m. last night for the new nest for Vanessa Sparrow. Owner of Nest for Avians, Vincent Vulture, stated that the nest will be installed in a tree near the Community Center. "This will allow Vanessa an easy commute to work as I know shows and events can go on late into the evening," said Vulture.

The nest was a cavity design with fresh grass flooring.

"I will never forget this day. In the words of Tanya Tucker, I have a 'mansion in the sky' now," said Vanessa.

Police Chief Millard Mallard has informed the Observer that all charges have been dropped in the

Restful Roost Community Center seed theft case against Vanessa Sparrow. "Vanessa has shown her true feathers in the recent days. She is actively participating in the community. I feel confident that dropping the charges is the right thing to do," said Chief Mallard.

rachel show is this evening! Don't forget your free ticket to the sold out show tonight if you helped out!

Goodbye 2022!

The *rachel* show was, as her name suggests, superb! Check out audio clips of the Superb Fairy Wren. You will not be disappointed! Vanessa seemed to be settling in nicely in Restful Roost. Charlene said Vanessa was a hard worker and very reliable. Charlene even hinted that she might have an opportunity to take a vacation in 2023 now that she has help. What a great way to end the year! The town overcame another attempted theft, helped out someone in need, celebrated a great show, and was rewarded with free healthcare.

Just another day in Restful Roost!

SPECIAL THANKS

Cornell Lab of Ornithology (Birdcast and All About Birds)

Birds' Eggs by Michael Walters

National Geographic Complete Birds of North America edited by Jonathan Alderfer

Peterson Field Guides *Eastern Birds' Nests* by Hal H. Harrison

My Pookie

Birds!

ABOUT THE AUTHOR

Susan is an investigative reporter with the Restful Roost Observer. She is an Eastern Towhee (Pipilo erythrophthalmus) and lives with her husband Adam Towhee in a quaint ground nest in the community of Restful Roost, TN. Susan is a founding board member of CFRR (Cat Free Restful Roost). She also enjoys bourbon, cigars, and cozy mysteries.